DEAR ADAM

KELSIE STELTING

For my dad. Thanks for
showing me how fun hard work can be.

CONTENTS

ONE

EMERICK

IF MRS. ARTHUR'S stupid bobbleheads kept nodding at me, I'd rip them in half.

Our guidance counselor had one from every college within a five-hundred-mile radius stacked in weird places—on top of papers, in the handles of her filing cabinets, on the ledge of the lone window in her office.

My mom hit my leg under the table. She didn't have to say anything for me to know what she meant. *Pay attention.*

I shook my own bobblehead and looked at Mrs. Arthur and our principal sitting on the opposite side of the table.

Mrs. Arthur leaned forward. "Unfortunately, you're a credit short, and all of our elective classes are full."

I hung my head. Yet another way I'd failed my mom. But working thirty hours a week on top of school made it hard to finish homework. Especially for idiotic classes like consumer math. I could use my freaking phone to do that math.

Mom worked her hands in her lap. "There has to be something he can do."

Mrs. Arthur exchanged glances with Principal Scott, and he nodded with his eyes closed like this was the least worthwhile thing he'd do all day.

She took in a deep breath. "You know about the *WAHS Ledger*?"

Mom shook her head, the lines around her eyes looking deeper than ever.

"It's the school's newspaper—an award-winning publication at that. I'm on the faculty editing board, and we believe there's one thing keeping us from placing at a national competition."

I raised my eyebrows. What did she think was missing? Actual news? Exposés on mystery meat weren't exactly hard-hitting stories.

Mrs. Arthur paused for dramatic effect. "We'd like to start up the advice column again. And we want it to be written by a guy."

Mom scoffed and sat back in her seat.

I didn't need her to say anything to understand that either.

Emerick is the last person who should be giving anyone advice.

And I agreed.

Apparently, Mrs. Arthur did, too, because she nodded. "Typically, we'd privately select someone from our journalism class, but seeing Emerick's predicament... Well, we'd like to give him a chance. Supervised, of course."

Mom took her purse from her chair and situated it over her shoulder. "He'll do it. What choice do we have?"

I looked from her to Mrs. Arthur. "Come on, there has to be something else. I wouldn't even know what to say to these preppy kids worrying about their hamsters dying."

Principal Scott leaned forward, the tips of his fingers tenting his hands on the table. "You will do it, and I think it would do you good to realize you're not the only one with problems."

I scowled at him. Yeah, other people might have to stress about what to wear or where to take a girl on a date, but I had real shit on my plate. Like basically a full-time job. Helping my mom save so we could move out of my uncle's house. A dad who couldn't help, not because he ran off, but because cops came to our shitty apartment and *took him away in handcuffs*.

Mom stood up and straightened the hem of her

scrub shirt. "You're absolutely right, Mr. Scott. If it's alright, will you sort the details with Emerick? I'm already late for my shift."

Principal Scott nodded. "Thanks for coming in, Mrs. Turner."

"Ms. Turner." Mom flashed him a come-get-me grin, and I almost vomited on the Pistol Pete bobble-head next to me. Seriously, Ma?

He straightened. "Ms. Turner. I can show you out. Mrs. Arthur, you'll get Emerick set up?"

She nodded. "Sure thing."

For the next hour, we talked about the advice column. Dear Adam—a spin on Dear Abby. She gave me a school laptop, an email address—dear-adam.WAHS@gmail.com—and directions to select three entries a week with responses to put in the paper.

"You can reply to just those three, or more if you'd like, but we have to have three in the paper each week."

"Sure." I folded my arms and leaned on the table. "There's just one problem."

She lifted her eyebrows. "What would that be?"

"I don't want to."

"At this point, it's this or drop out." She stood up and walked back to her desk. "The choice is up to you."

I shoved the laptop in my messenger bag and picked up my leather jacket from where it rested over my chair.

"Good choice," she said.

I gave her a final look and walked out of that office. And right into my worst nightmare.

TWO

NORA

I SLAMMED into a wall of muscle and leather and teen angst. My note cards flew through the air and landed on the ground beside me.

"Ouch." I rubbed my elbow. I'd told my mom heels weren't a good idea, but it turned out Emerick Turner was my worst fall risk.

He sat back on the floor like he belonged there. Like we didn't have a school assembly in five minutes. "You alright?"

I trained my eyes on the ground as my dad's voice played in the back of my mind. *Everyone should feel like you like them, no matter what.* That was going to be hard.

"I'm fine," I said and started gathering my note cards.

A hand came under my arm. "Babe, you alright?"

Trey—Walter Evans III, but Trey—hauled me to my feet, and I pulled my arm from his grip. I wasn't his "babe." Not anymore.

"I'm fine," I repeated, more forcefully this time.

A few note cards held by an oil-stained hand came into my vision. I glanced up—Emerick. "Thanks." I took them from him.

He lifted a dark eyebrow in response and turned away so all we could see was the back of his worn leather jacket and his easy saunter as he walked away.

I tore my gaze from him and started straightening my A-line skirt and cardigan. A button had come undone when I fell. I didn't want to look messy for my first speech of the semester. I only had a few months left in my term as student body president, and I wasn't going to waste it.

"That guy's a jerk," Trey said.

I sorted my note cards in order by the numbers I'd written in the bottom corners. Another tip from my dad. "Ready?"

Trey nodded. "Do you want to run through your talk?"

"I'm perfectly capable. You, on the other hand..."

He gripped his chest, feigning pain. "I only threw up one time. And that was last year."

"It's January."

His lips spread into an easy grin. The one that got him whatever he wanted. "You got me."

I shook my head but kept my chin high. We were getting closer to the gym. *Don't display anything other than confidence. People can smell fear, weakness.*

Students were still filtering in, but I kept my back straight and mingled with people as we walked into the gym, making sure to say hi to everyone I knew. To say something personal. *How's your sister? What was England like at Christmastime? How did you manage to break your nose and both wrists snowboarding?* That kind of thing.

Trey and I made it to the first bleacher row and sat down. He was so close his shoulder brushed mine. I scooted a couple of inches away.

He gave me a look, but he wouldn't say something in front of the entire student body. I'd hear about it later.

Principal Scott started the assembly with the usual housekeeping stuff and a speech about how excited he was to be in the final stretch of the school year. As he spoke, I found myself critiquing his performance. Didn't he know you weren't supposed to say "um" more than five times in a minute?

Finally, it was my turn.

My heels clacked against the finished gym floor

until I stood behind the podium, staring out at the entire student body—my friends, my ex, even Emerick, who was whispering and joking with one of his friends. The smile that crossed his face was a rare one, and the way it transformed his features was like magic.

"Miss Wilson?"

I gave my head a quick shake and looked back at Principal Scott, trying to hide how frazzled I was. Was I seriously daydreaming about Emerick Turner in front of all of WAHS?

I shook the thought and started talking, hardly glancing at my note cards. This was where I belonged. In front of a crowd. Helping them make this school an even better place to be a student.

"That is why we're enacting a mental health initiative here at school," I said. "Homeroom on Fridays will be dedicated to a mindfulness practice. There will now be pamphlets in Principal Scott's office highlighting everything from how to handle bullies to how to talk with your parents about sex. And, something we're really excited about, there will be a change to the school's newspaper."

Sure, the students acted like they couldn't have cared less, but I'd done my research. This would be a good thing.

High with the energy from speaking and finally

seeing my ideas come into action, I grinned at Trey and waved him forward.

He came to stand beside me at the podium. "Hi there, WAHS!"

The student body clapped excitedly. Everyone loved Trey. Everyone but me.

In a fake show of humility, he bowed his head. "Oh, stop it."

They quieted, and he went on.

"As editor of the *WAHS Ledger*, I've been working tirelessly to make sure we bring home another national newspaper title. But we've been missing one thing: an advice column. We know it might be a little awkward asking for help, so we're creating a one hundred percent confidential portal where you can email our advice columnist. Several of the questions will be published in our paper each week with coun-selor-reviewed advice."

While the crowd clapped, Trey ducked his head and stepped back, sans puke. He must have been practicing.

I moved forward again. "Mrs. Arthur has some announcements next. But thank you so much for making WAHS awesome. Let's bring in the end of the school year with a bang!"

After the assembly, my two best friends came to

find me and looped their arms through each of mine. I loved it when we walked like this—it reminded me of third grade and sleepovers and times when my biggest worry was whether a boy checked yes or no. Grace and London had been there for it all.

Grace jiggled my arm. "You did awesome, girl. You're totally gonna take over the world someday."

I chuckled. "I think I'll leave that to Dad."

London shrugged. "As long as you promise to pardon all my speeding tickets."

I raised my eyebrows. "People might start getting suspicious after the tenth time."

She laughed. "I've only had three."

Grace nodded. "Yeah, but you've been pulled over seven more times than that and somehow talked them out of it."

London batted her eyelashes. "Pure talent."

We got a little closer to my first period class. "I better get going."

Grace dropped her arm from mine. "Hang out after practice?"

She managed the basketball team, and London was a cheerleader. We almost never had enough time to hang out on school nights.

I shook my head. "Nah, I've got volunteer hours to do."

Looking perfectly pouty, London said, "Fine, but we're hanging out this weekend. No buts."

I smiled. We'd see about that.

After school, I loaded my backpack into my car. I didn't have volunteer hours. I had to go buy groceries for my family.

THREE
EMERICK

"YOU'VE gotta start thinking about what you want to do with your life, Rick," Uncle Ken said over the sounds of drills and engines.

I wiped sweat from my forehead and stared down at the tire I was working on patching. Were we really on this again? But this wasn't exactly the kind of conversation we could have at his house, where my mom and I lived with him, his wife, and my three cousins.

"Emerick..."

I sighed. "You know I can't leave Ma."

Uncle Ken rubbed a grease-stained rag over his hands. "We'll take care of her. You know that."

"Yeah, but will she let you?"

He shook his head, not in the "no" way, but in the

exasperated way. We both knew Mom could hardly handle being alone. If she didn't have me around, she'd go off and find some guy to fill the empty spot in her heart—and her bank account. And judging by my father, the felon, she didn't have the greatest taste in men.

I just had to get enough saved up for a down payment on a little house for us. Something with a mortgage small enough for her to handle if she ever had to be without me. And when I didn't have school to worry about, it would be way easier to save up.

But I had a lot of work to do before then.

"You gonna let me bust this tire?" I asked.

Uncle Ken clapped my shoulder, a heavy look in his eyes. "Just think about it."

I nodded.

Honestly, it was all I could think about. One of his best mechanics, Bernie, was retiring soon. I hadn't gone to school for it or anything, but I'd learned enough from work that I could step in. It was decent money—full-time work that wasn't in the oil fields. Uncle Ken would give me the job, but I couldn't tell whether he actually wanted me to take it or not.

Aunt Linda came over at five with their three kids and food. The younger two ran back along the edge of the shop to his office, but the oldest, Janie, came over to me.

"Whatcha working on?" she asked, standing on her tiptoes. She was ten and still really short. How tall were ten-year-olds supposed to be, though?

I gestured at the tire spinning in front of me. "You've seen me patch tires before."

She nodded, her little beaded braids crackling.

"How was school?" I asked.

She lifted her bony shoulders. "I punched Johnny Andrews in the gut."

I fought an amused smile. "Yeah?"

"Yep." She nodded. "Kept my thumb outside my fist like you taught me."

My eyes widened, and I looked around to make sure no one heard me. "That's between us, right?" I waited for her to nod before saying, "So that little punk pretended your hair was an abacus again?"

She rolled her eyes. "Three times. I warned him, like you told me to."

I folded my arms across my chest. "Well, he deserved it then, huh?"

"Tell Mom that."

"You in trouble?" I asked.

A small smile spread across her lips. "Not this time."

"And it won't happen again, right?"

She grinned. "He cried. I don't think so."

That time, I couldn't keep from laughing. I put

my fist out, she bumped her knuckles against mine, and then we exploded our fingers back. Yeah, I had a secret handshake with a ten-year-old. Sue me.

"Janie!" Aunt Linda called from the office. "Rick! You eatin'?"

"Yeah!" we yelled back at the same time.

My shift got over at ten, but I ended up staying until 10:45, thanks to that one asshole who always walks in right at closing time. But I needed the money, and the guy had a flat.

After work, I walked home. The shop was only about a mile from Uncle Ken's house, and by the time I got there, I could hardly feel my fingers. Leather jackets? Sturdy, not exactly cozy.

I took a quick shower—Aunt Linda would kill me if I got grease on her sheets—and then I went to the garage they'd converted into a bedroom for me. Meaning, they'd put a futon and a space heater out there, along with their washer and dryer, the mower, lawn fertilizer, hoses, and a power washer.

I couldn't complain. It wasn't much worse than the little apartment we used to live in where I slept on the couch and Ma and Dad—when he was around —took the bedroom. At least I had a little privacy now.

I dropped down on the futon and pulled the

laptop Mrs. Arthur gave me from my bag. It was one of the school's old, clunky ones. I lifted the screen up, logged in, and typed in Uncle Ken's Wi-Fi password. Mrs. Arthur had already logged me into the Dear Adam gmail account.

There were a few spam emails—anyone want to make friends with a prince from Nigeria? But then there were also a few real messages.

From: WAHS Portal [Long-term Girlfriend]
To: DEAR ADAM

Dear Adam,

I've been dating the same guy for a long time, and now that we're seniors, I'm wondering if we should keep dating? We'll be going to college soon, and everyone's telling me that's the best time of your life to make friends and date new guys and that having a boyfriend in college will just hold me back. I love him, but is that enough?

Long-term Girlfriend

I sighed at the screen and ran my hand over my tight curls. Whose idiotic idea was it to have me write this? Had they just looked for the least qualified person for the job and zoned in on me? I didn't have time for a relationship—let alone helping other people with theirs. But there were so many times I'd wanted to tell my mom what to do in *her* relationships. Maybe this was my chance to share the advice I never could give her.

I opened up a new email, addressed to Mrs. Arthur, and wrote my first column.

Dear Long-term Girlfriend,

You say you love him, but do you? If you really liked this dude, breaking up wouldn't even be on your mind. I think the fact that you're wondering about it is answer enough. Just let him down easy. And not in a text. That's just uncool.

Signed,
Adam

I created a new folder in my account and moved that email to "Done." On to the next one.

From: WAHS Portal {2 Young}
To: DEAR ADAM
Dear Adam,

I'm a freshman, and a senior guy asked me out. When I told my parents about it, they flipped. Like, my dad literally lost it, saying I'm too young to date and that senior guys only have one thing on their mind. But I feel really pissed because, well, that means he doesn't trust me to pick which guys to date. That's absolute crap. How can I get my dad to see that it's time to let me choose who I want to go out with?

Sincerely,
2 Young

I dragged my hand over my face. Was graduating really worth it?

Ma would kill me if I didn't though. Literally.

Dear 2 Young,

The term "fresh-meat freshman" exists for a reason. And your dad? Might not be too far off base. I mean, unless you've been in a guys' locker room, it's kinda hard to understand where your old man's coming from. But if you're super set on dating this guy, maybe ask for supervised dates? If this dude's not just in it for one thing, he wouldn't mind having your parents tag along to the movies or something.

Signed,
Adam

My eyes already felt tired from staring at the computer screen, but I went on to the next email. There were five, and I only needed three. Maybe I could knock this one out and not have to worry about it for the rest of the week.

From: WAHS Portal [Setting Things Straight]
To: DEAR ADAM
Dear Adam,

I don't even know why I'm writing you. I guess I just feel hopeless at this point. I came out to my parents last week, and my mom hasn't talked to me since then. Hasn't even looked at me. We used to talk all the time, and now I feel like she wouldn't even care if I just left and didn't come back. I don't know what to do to make things right.

Love,
Setting Things Straight

My gut hurt like I'd eaten something bad. That story hit too close to home. Yeah, I wasn't gay or anything, but having a parent treat you like you didn't exist? I got that.

Dear Setting Things Straight,

That sucks. Even though I can't totally relate, not feeling accepted as who you are is the worst feeling ever. If you were brave enough to be honest with them, you're tough enough to get through this too. And, take it from me, not all parents are who you thought they'd be. That's on them, though. Not you.

Signed,
Adam

As I typed the words, hit save, and closed the laptop, I wondered how much I believed that last part. If at all.

FOUR

NORA

I WAS TRYING to do some last-minute review for the American Government test, but everyone in our class was talking too loudly. Some guys a few rows over were seeing whether they could throw grapes in the air and catch them in their mouths. These girls right next to me were talking about date ideas. Usually, I was good at tuning everything out—living with four younger siblings teaches you that real quick —but they said something about the school newspaper, and I had to listen.

"Did you read that advice column?" one girl whispered to her friends.

I kept my gaze down so they couldn't tell I was eavesdropping, but I saw the other two nod out of my periphery.

One of them giggled. "That thing he wrote to the

girl whose boyfriend started baby talking to her? Classic."

Her friend laughed. "Right? Or what about the one from the kid coming out?"

The other girls nodded solemnly.

"He just...gets it, you know? It's not all preachy like a lot of columns."

Despite myself, I smiled. The advice column had been a great idea, and whoever Adam was, he was doing a great job. His identity had been kept totally secret. Trey actually seemed pretty miffed that the newspaper teacher wouldn't tell him who Adam was. But for the column to work, people had to trust who they wrote to, even if it meant messaging a complete stranger.

I looked up from my notes and caught sight of Emerick a few rows over. He was leaned back in his chair, head tilted back, talking to one of his friends behind him. For the briefest seconds, our eyes caught. He arched an eyebrow, like he was saying, what? But not in a helpful way. Maybe in a challenging way?

I didn't know. Eyebrows shouldn't need translators. And I shouldn't have been so curious about what his meant.

Our teacher started talking about the test, and I directed my attention back toward the material. I pored over every line of my notes I could until he asked us to clear our desks.

The rest of the day passed as usual, and I hurried to the parking lot after school to meet my sister. Since she was only a freshman and didn't have her permit, she needed me to take her to her dance lesson across town.

She was already waiting at the car when I arrived, her toe tapping like I was late.

I ignored the toe, got in, and we left the parking lot. I tried talking to her on the way, but she was writing on a notebook in her lap, trying to get some homework done.

After dropping her off, I drove to Warr Acres City Hall. I interned there one day a week—mostly doing paperwork—but Dad promised me working in government at a young age would pay off down the road. He said starting later in life hurt him in his race for mayor of the city and now in his attempt at governor. But for how much he worked, how much he was away from home, he deserved the position. All of us did for having to pick up the slack while he was gone.

By the time I picked Amie up and drove home, I was exhausted and nursing more than a few paper cuts. Plus, I still had an AP English assignment to do.

Food. Then homework. Amie and I trudged inside toward the kitchen, and I stopped short.

Trey was sitting at the table with Mom and my youngest sister, chatting like nothing had ever happened between us.

Mom looked up at me and grinned. "You have a visitor, Nora."

I smiled, but my lips felt tight.

She stood from the table. "I already made supper. Why don't you two take it upstairs?"

As Mom turned away to get the plates, I gave Trey a look that I hoped said, *what the h-e-double-hockey-sticks are you doing here, you scumbag?*

Trey replied with an *I'm an idiot* shrug. But when Mom turned back to us, he replaced his even expression with a warm smile.

"Thanks, Mrs. Wilson." He eyed the plate full of mashed potatoes and gravy and salmon. "Man, I've missed your cooking."

She set the food on the table and put her free hand over her heart. "You flatter me, Trey."

Of course he did—that was Trey's specialty. Actually putting any meaning behind his words? Well, that was a different story.

I picked up my dish from the island and turned to go upstairs. "Come on."

"Remember to keep your door open," Mom said, already focusing on my little sister.

Trey's voice dripped with that perfect-teen-boy

kindness parents ate up. "Of course, Mrs. Wilson."

I hurried up the stairs, not worried about whether he was following.

Of course, he was right behind me when I walked into my room, and he sat in my desk chair like he belonged there.

I set my plate on the dresser and whirled to face him. There had to be at least one exception to Dad's kindness rule, and he was sitting right in front of me. "What are you doing here?"

He took a bite of potatoes and took his time chewing, even though someone with dentures could have eaten the goop quicker than Trey.

"I wanted to talk to you," he said, carefully cutting his salmon.

"Well, you better hurry. I have a paper to write for English, and I have to help Mom with Amie's costume. Oh, and I need to sleep." I definitely did not have time for this.

Trey turned his soft hazel eyes on me, the eyes I'd fallen in love with when we worked the junior prom committee together. "Nora, just hear me out."

I grabbed my plate from the dresser, dropped onto my bed, and shoveled some flaky salmon into my mouth.

"That's not very ladylike."

I rolled my eyes.

He chuckled. "You're so cute when you do that."

Okay, now I was fuming. I swallowed. "Get to the point, Trey."

"Look." He reached into his pocket and pulled out a small brooch.

My eyes flew to the delicate gold flower. "Is that..." I reached out to touch it.

"Your grandma's," he finished. "I found it at a pawn shop the other day."

I looked up into those eyes and then back at the only thing I had left of my grandma. She'd given it to me to wear at prom, right before she passed away. I clutched it to my chest and closed my eyes. My heart had been broken without it.

He cleared his throat. "I...um, I've been looking for it ever since you lost it, and I guess I just got lucky."

I met his eyes again. "Thank you."

The corner of his mouth pulled back in a half smile. "Anything for you. You know that."

Did I?

"Nora, I..." His eyes turned down. "I'm sorry I broke up with you."

I squeezed my eyes shut. This? Now? "It's fine."

His hand felt heavy on my shoulder. "It wasn't. It's not. I made a huge mistake."

I blinked at him, eyes wide, and not because he

was wearing a tight T-shirt that showed off his basketball muscles or because he wore my favorite cologne of his, but because I wanted to believe that was true.

But I couldn't. "I thought you said you didn't want to date someone long distance?"

"Yeah, it's going to be hard when you're at OU and I'm at Columbia, but we'll make it work, right? There are video calls and email and text. And month-long winter breaks. And it would probably be better if we weren't a distraction to each other while we're in school anyway."

"A distraction?" Was that how he saw me?

"You know what I mean." He ran his thumb over the cap of my shoulder, and it sent shivers to my stomach. "We always agreed school came first."

"Yeah, and that's why we hardly had time to hang out when we were dating," I reminded him.

His hand dropped from my shoulder to my waist. "I thought our study dates were fun." He wiggled his eyebrows.

I batted his hand away, but I couldn't help but smile. Kissing with our books open had been a really nice way to study. That was the closest I'd ever come to getting a B, though.

He came a little closer and twirled a piece of my hair in his fingers. "I'd do anything for you." One of his hands covered mine, the one that was holding my grandma's brooch. "Just think about it. Promise?"

I sighed and closed my eyes. "I promise."

He left down the stairs, showing himself out like he had so many times before.

But the problem was, I didn't have time to think about this. I barely had time to write my paper. Which, for the record, I did. Just not very well. Then I went downstairs and helped Mom pin and sew on pieces of Amie's dance costume. And then, when one of the babies started crying, I went to her room and fed her a bottle. And then, when I fell into bed, totally exhausted, with only six hours before school started the next day, I was still thinking about Trey.

So, I reached out to the only person I could think of.

Adam.

FIVE
EMERICK

I WAS ABOUT to close my laptop when a new email flashed across the screen. Even though not every question got put into the newspaper, I read them all. It was kind of like watching the *Jerry Springer Show*—seeing how many problems everyone else had made me feel a little less bad about my own.

Seriously, if you looked at the social media accounts of the kids at my school, you'd think they lived the perfect lives, went on vacations all the time, or always hung out with friends. But these letters told me something different. I'd gotten at least a hundred of them already, and they didn't show any signs of slowing down.

I told myself I'd read just one more before going to bed and clicked open the newest email.

From: WAHS Portal [ThePerfectStranger]
To: DEAR ADAM

Dear Adam,

I hope you're having a nice evening. I want to start this by saying I don't want my email in the paper. I just...wanted to talk to someone who might understand. Someone who might give me some clue of what to do. I know you probably get a lot of emails, so if you don't have time for mine, I understand.

I guess I'll just jump in. I met this guy last year, and we started dating at prom. Everything seemed perfect. My parents loved him, we had a lot of the same goals for our future, he got along with my younger siblings... He was perfect, basically. I won't bore you with how cute he is, but, trust me, he's not bad to look at, either.

But when we started getting acceptance letters back from college, things changed. He applied to schools out of state, and I didn't. I couldn't leave if I wanted to. My family needs me here to help. But he doesn't get that. He told me I was throwing my life away by not seeing the world and that he didn't want to have a long-distance relationship. So, we broke up. Well, he broke up with me. And it hurt. But he just asked me out again, and I'm not sure what to say.

The thing is, I don't think anyone even knows we're broken up. We still hang out together at school all the time. He drops by my house. He still calls me babe in front of other people. But now? I don't know if I even want to be in a relationship with him. Do I want to date someone who is always going to put school and work first? Is it something he'll grow out of?

I'm realizing I basically sent you a novel, so I'm sorry. You can reply to my email if you want. It's theperfect-stranger12@gmail.com.

ThePerfectStranger

PS – I read about something called "Caregiver's Fatigue." Basically, it's like the people who are always helping others need help too. So if you ever want to talk, I'm here.

PSS – I'm hearing great things about your column. Keep up the good work.

That email had me all over the place—smiling, feeling bad, feeling surprised. I'd gotten a lot of emails, but none of them had ever asked how I was doing with everything or offered help. But the thing that stood out most in her email? Needing to stay around her family. I got that. The feeling of family over everything else—even your future.

So, for the first time, I wrote back. Not for the paper, just for her.

From: ADAM
To: ThePerfectStranger
Hey ThePerfectStranger,

I'm having a good evening, thanks for asking, and don't worry about the email. A little light reading never hurt anyone. Just don't tell Ms. Chance I said that.

I guess if you wanted advice, you came to the right guy. But you're not going to get the benefit of this going through the counselor, so I guess you're stuck with me. If that's okay. Tell me to stop whenever.

First off, I think it's pretty awesome you're putting your family first. It isn't easy to sacrifice your own dreams when you have other people around pushing you in the other direction. If this guy really got you and your family, why would he say you're throwing your life away? Wouldn't he understand?

The worst part about writing an advice column is that I can't get clarification, but since I have your email...I have some questions of my own. What did he say when he asked you back? Did he have any excuses? What makes you think he won't just dump you the second he goes off to college?

And I think there's a bigger question here. Do you want him back?

Signed,
Adam

PS – Thank you.

PSS – Also, thank you.

Even though I waited for another half hour, ThePerfectStranger didn't reply. But I was so exhausted, sleep came easily. When I opened my eyes again, it was time to get ready for school.

I got up from the futon, brought my clothes to the bathroom, and showered up. I always got up earlier than everyone else because Uncle Ken and Aunt Linda only had one bathroom and three kids. I loved Janie, but that girl could get vicious if she didn't have time to sing in the shower.

After I got out, I went to the kitchen to help Aunt Linda cook breakfast. Between the two of us, we had a pretty good routine going.

She kissed me on the cheek. "Can you make the eggs today?"

I nodded. "Burnt scrambles it is."

She shoved my shoulder, and I chuckled under my breath. While she made coffee and ran in and out of the kitchen to yell at the kids to get ready, I cooked up some eggs covered in sliced cheese.

Mom came into the kitchen, and I passed her a plate. She scarfed it down and headed out the door, already wearing her scrubs.

Aunt Linda went to the corner of the kitchen and hollered at Uncle Ken in the boys' room. "Make sure those boys have socks on and get in here for breakfast!"

Their house was so loud in the mornings, not like our quiet apartment when Mom and I stayed with

Dad. They were always gone. My aunt and uncle's house was full of noise and energy and fighting, but the good kind.

Janie skipped to the breakfast table, and I set a plate of eggs and toast in front of her. "Bon appetit."

She eyed her plate, then gave me a skeptical look. "Bones?"

Aunt Linda laughed. "It's French."

"These eggs don't look French."

I laughed too. "It means 'eat up.'"

"Oh." She shrugged and dug in.

Aunt Linda and I smiled at each other. Linda wasn't a classically pretty lady—actually, I was pretty sure she wore a wig—but she had a big smile and a deep laugh that made everything seem less serious. I could tell why Uncle Ken married her.

Uncle Ken came to the table with two very sleepy looking seven-year-olds and sat down. Aunt Linda and I plated some food for them, then I sat, as well.

My aunt put a hand on Janie's arm, stalling her total devastation of the eggs I'd cooked. "No fighting today, right?"

Janie looked toward the sky. "Mom, it's been a week."

"And tomorrow it better be a week and a day, you got me?"

Janie looked at me, and I winked at her. She was fighting a smile when she mumbled, "Alright, alright."

A honk came from outside.

"That's Wolf," I said and scarfed down the last of my eggs.

I jogged to the garage and grabbed my bag, then ran out to the driveway where my friend sat in his El Camino. It was kind of a lame car that was broken down just as often as it ran, but I wasn't going to complain about having a ride to school.

I threw my bag through the window, then dropped into his seat. As he pulled down the street, black smoke sputtered out behind us.

"You got work this weekend?" he asked.

I nodded. "Yeah, why?"

He shook his head, but his stringy hair barely moved. "Got a gig Saturday night. You down?"

"Where?" Wolf's band always got hooked up at these weird hole-in-the-wall joints where I usually got in, even though I wasn't twenty-one.

"Ottos. On the east side of town."

"Near Midwest City?"

He nodded.

I shrugged. "Yeah, I'm down."

What else did I have to do?

We pulled up in the school parking lot and walked

past all the jocks sitting around in the back of some pickup playing country music.

"Look who showed up to school," the ringleader yelled. The student body vice president himself. "It's dog and his bitch."

My brows furrowed. Seriously?

Wolf squared his shoulders. "Where's your sister? Shouldn't you be making out or something?"

I had to hand it to Wolf. He wasn't afraid to dish it back. The only problem was this guy had fifty pounds on Wolf and hours of weightlifting behind him.

I grabbed Wolf's shoulder and kept walking.

But the guy yelled back, "That's cute. Take care of your woman, faggot."

I shot him a hard stare but kept walking.

We got several feet away, and Wolf seemed to relax.

"Trash," Wolf muttered, but I didn't say anything back. He just needed to get it out.

Those jocks just liked to cause problems because they wouldn't get in trouble if we had a fight. The principal would just see some rich white kid with decent grades and parents in the PTA who got caught up in problems with some poor black guy barely passing with a convict father. Oh, yeah, and his drug-dabbling friend. The odds were not in our favor.

We made it to the lockers, and I nodded at him. "Catch you Saturday?"

He straightened his coat. "Yeah."

Wolf was probably going to skip today, but I went to all of my classes. It wasn't that I wanted to, but you should have seen the look on my mother's face when Principal Scott called and said I might not graduate. I'd do anything not to see her that disappointed ever again.

I was surprised when Wolf actually showed up to social studies. And glad, because Mr. Roberts said he had a partner project for us.

But then Mr. Roberts said the most dreaded words surrounding partner projects: "I've assigned you into pairs."

I didn't think it could get any worse, but then he called my name along with Nora Wilson. Student body president. Daughter of the dude who was probably going to be Oklahoma's governor. Total snob.

Yeah, she was a smoke show, but her personality ruined it. And the way she looked down her nose at me pretty much said she felt the same way.

SIX

NORA

I STARED at my future project partner. Seriously? Couldn't Mr. Roberts have paired me up with anyone else? I would have taken anyone—even the kid who had such sensitive skin he couldn't wear deodorant. Even the girl who drew pentagrams and tried to summon ghosts in her free time. But here I was.

Mr. Roberts told us to change seats so we were sitting next to our partners. Emerick sat there like he was waiting for me to move, but I folded my arms over my chest and leaned back. He could come to me.

His lips twitched like he couldn't tell whether to smile or grimace, and he slid out of his desk to come my way.

While Mr. Roberts talked about the assignment— learning about elections and creating a campaign plan

—I noticed Emerick's hands. They were big, strong, and he kept his nails short. His ebony skin met his paler skin in a line at his palms. And there was that grease again. Up close, I could tell they were clean, just stained. Did he work in a shop?

I didn't have time to think about it, because Mr. Roberts was handing out a thick assignment package. Emerick kept his hands on the desk like he knew I'd want to take it. Well, he was right.

I studied the rubric on top and internally groaned. We had to present an update on our plan each Friday, we'd need to host elections in the school with primaries and all, and we'd eventually have to speak at a debate in front of the entire student body. Oh, and we'd have to send invitations to parents. Great.

"We should be set," Emerick said, close to my ear.

I jumped. He was reading over my shoulder. "Running for student body president was enough. I don't want to do it again."

His full lips curled. "Yeah, but can't we just take your dad's strategy?"

I looked toward the ceiling. "Some of us might be okay with cheating"—I gave him a pointed look —"but I'm not."

Emerick sat back, folding his arms over his chest. "You sayin' I'm a cheater?"

I looked toward the paper. "And we have a field trip."

He chuckled low. "This is gonna be a fun semester."

Sarcasm. That, I could relate to. "The best."

I flipped through a few more of the pages. This project would be intense, and I didn't have the time to do it on my own. I shifted in my seat and looked him straight in the eyes—leveled with him.

"Look," I said. "I need a partner. A real partner. And I don't need someone who's going to slack off and not do their part. So if you're hoping you're going to be paired up with someone who's just going to do everything, you need to go ask Mr. Roberts for a new partner right now."

Emerick leaned forward, resting one arm on the desk and the other on his knee. These desks were too small for him. But the look in his eyes got me. The pained, frustrated look that made his dark eyes seem heavier.

"You have this idea of me, and you don't even know me."

He said it like a fact, and I bristled. "You're telling me you don't think of me as some entitled rich girl?"

"Bingo, let's get this girl a prize. It'll be waiting in your brand-new crossover sitting in the parking lot."

My eyes narrowed. That thing had come with a

price—giving up my life to haul my siblings around, step in when Dad had to be gone campaigning. But Emerick wouldn't understand that.

"So then, we're on the same page," I said and inclined my head toward the teacher's desk. "Are you asking him, or am I?"

Emerick sat back in his chair like he was lounging in his living room and folded his arms across his broad chest. "I'm not backing down." He lifted his eyebrows in Mr. Roberts's direction. "Go on. Let's see how this goes."

I clenched my fists under my desk. He was infuriating! I didn't know whether to hit something or scream—neither of which I did on a regular basis. Dealing with my toddler sisters was easier than this.

"You going?" he pressed.

My lips formed a tight line. I was not backing down from this challenge either. Because going to Mr. Roberts would mean he'd won, and I wasn't a loser. Not when I ran for student body president. Not when dealing with some cocky greaser with a Texas-sized chip on his shoulder.

I flashed him one of my presidential grins. "Nope. We're going to have a great semester."

His lips twitched, and his eyes took on an amused expression. "I bet."

For the rest of class, Emerick and I planned out

the semester according to the rubric. Well, I made plans, and he made wisecracks. But a couple of times he pointed things out that I missed.

He wasn't dumb. Just unmotivated, which was just as bad.

After class, I loaded up my backpack and walked out of the classroom without saying goodbye.

Trey caught up to me. "You got stuck with Turner." He laughed. "That suuuucks."

I glared at him. "Not in the mood."

He changed tactics, reaching around my backpack and rubbing my shoulder. "When's Amie's next recital?"

"Why don't you ask her?"

"Whoa." He lifted his hands.

Taking in a deep breath, I turned my head down. "Sorry. Sorry. It's just been a rough day."

He took my hand in his and stopped so I had to stand still with him in the hallway while students walked all around us. It was like he was trying to pull me back into our old bubble. The one where I'd only been able to see us—the only two people in the world. But that bubble had popped the second he'd ended it.

"Nora," he said, his voice low and smooth. "You know you don't have to do this all by yourself, right? I'm here for you."

I looked down at our hands. At his that were soft and stain-free. Those hands were great at handling basketballs, but were his days of handling me over?

"Thanks." I sighed. "I have to get to class. Talk to you later?"

His lips tugged into a smile. "Yeah." He tucked my hair behind my ear, and his touch felt warm, familiar. And then he left, lost in the sea of students.

The after-school rush continued. I took Amie to dance, then drove to the hospital. I volunteered there, giving people directions, helping get drinks and things like that. Tonight it was really slow, which, while technically a good thing, I was bored.

I took my phone out of my purse and checked my new email account. One email from Adam. My heart pounded. When I'd sent the message, I really hadn't expected to hear back, especially not so soon.

I read his words, and my breath caught in my chest. I didn't know what I'd been hoping for, but this was...a lot to take in. His questions—they were a lot. *What did he say when he asked you back? Did he have any excuses? What makes you think he won't just dump you the second he goes off to college? And I think there's a bigger question here. Do you want him back?*

He also asked why Trey didn't get it that I needed to stay with my family. That might have been the hardest question to answer.

I looked around. The lobby was completely empty. The security guard next to me clicked away at the computer, losing at a game of solitaire. So, I hit reply.

From: The Perfect Stranger
To: ADAM

Dear Adam,

Thank you so much for messaging me. I'm sure you have your plate full with classwork and the column. I know I do. I never thought too much about you needing to ask clarification questions, but I'm glad you could write back.

Your first question, about why he doesn't understand...I don't know. He's the youngest of two children in his family, and I think everything's always been taken care of for him. He never had to worry about things other than just being a kid, I guess. Honestly, I don't even know if he knows how to do laundry. He'll probably hire someone to do it when he goes to college. Maybe he just thinks my parents would step up if I left, but the thing is that they can't. I have several younger sisters, and my dad is gone all the time. There's no way Mom could handle the youngest two full-time, my sister in middle school, and my sister in high school. I'm the only other one old enough to drive. What's she supposed to do? Uber my siblings everywhere?

When he asked me back, he gave me something of my grandma's that I'd lost. It was a really precious family heirloom. And he said he would be there for me, that we would work it out, and that it might even be better if we were long distance in college because then we wouldn't be around to distract each other all the time. I know that doesn't sound very romantic, but, let's face it. Between classes and family obligations and extracurriculars, we hardly have time for each other as it is. It's better that one of us won't feel left out.

And do I want him back? I don't know, otherwise I wouldn't be writing you. Part of me wants to say yes. Dating him had been like a dream—I always felt like we were the couple that was going somewhere. But then he ended things so easily.

I'm the kind of person who always makes the "right" decision. My parents can rely on me, and my friends think I'm a prude. The fact that I don't know what to do now is killing me, and I feel so much pressure to just make a good decision, but I don't know how. I guess I'll get back to you on that one.

Do you ever feel like you won't know if something is a bad idea or not until you actually try it?

ThePerfectStranger

PS – It's weird saying all of this to a stranger. Maybe you should tell me about yourself?

I deleted and retyped that last line at least three times, but someone walked into the lobby and I hit send. The question just happened to still be there.

After helping a soon-to-be dad find the maternity ward, I clocked out, hung up my volunteer badge, and went to my car. I picked Amie up from the dance studio, and we drove home in a tired silence. For all the time we spent together, it seemed like we hardly talked.

"Any plans this weekend?" I tried.

She glanced at me. "You mean other than helping Mom change diapers?"

I snorted. "Yeah, in addition to that."

She shrugged. "Dad wouldn't let me go on that date, so not really. Maybe go see Chels."

Her best friend lived only a few houses away, and they hung out almost constantly until Amie started competitive ballet and had four-hour practices every day. If she played her cards right, she could be dancing for the Oklahoma City Ballet full-time in less than a couple of years.

"Are you seeing Trey?" she asked.

My lips wavered. Faking a smile was difficult this late in the day. "Maybe."

I waited for her to ask me something else, but she just leaned her head back and rested her eyes until we got to the house.

At least since it was late, the younger three were already in bed. I hopped in the shower, finished up a worksheet for my science class, and opened my computer to one new email from Adam.

SEVEN

EMERICK

THEPERFECTSTRANGER WROTE ME BACK, and I didn't know why I cared so much. I didn't even have to respond to her. Technically, I was only in it for three answers a week. I never got to hear back from the people I wrote to, though. Yeah, I heard people talk about the column from time to time at school, but that wasn't the same as having a conversation with someone.

I read through her email, hating her ex even though I didn't know him. From what she wrote, she was running ragged taking care of herself and her family. How could he say he cared about her and not understand it? But then again, I didn't have a girl-friend. Who was I to talk?

From: ADAM
To: ThePerfectStranger

You know you don't have to keep thanking me, right? It's kind of my job to write this column. And you're giving me tons of great practice. Just kidding. But really, it's fine.

I guess it's hard for me to understand where he's coming from. Ever since my dad left, I felt like I had to be around for my mom. I couldn't imagine moving away from her. (Okay, is that enough personal detail?) Do you think you could just talk with this guy and explain to him what's going on if you haven't already? Maybe he just needs it spelled out in plain English. Guys can be a little slow sometimes, you know.

And you're right, having a long-distance boyfriend just because you don't have time for one IRL doesn't sound romantic. Are you sure you both shouldn't just take time for yourselves? I mean, what's the point in dating if you can't drag them along to family things? Or at least have someone to hang out with on the weekends?

I know a little something about expectations. It's like when people see you, they don't even see a person.

They just see a history, a set of decisions, and they expect everything you do in the future to line up with what you've done in the past. I guess it makes sense, but still, sometimes it would be nice to just be able to make a decision without having to disappoint someone or live up to what they think of you.

Signed,
Adam

PS – I kind of agree. What do you want to know?

Seeing the look of disappointment on Nora Wilson's face when Mr. Roberts announced me as her lab partner was just another reminder of who people thought I was. And yeah, I had slacked on group projects before, but I wasn't stupid. Just busy. And dealing with shit other kids had no idea about. You ever see your dad get dragged away from the house in handcuffs and watch the cops rip a necklace off your mom's neck because it was stolen? Yeah, I didn't think so.

I clicked through a few other messages, hoping ThePerfectStranger would reply. If I was being honest, I didn't really talk to anyone. Wolf and I mostly talked about cars or girls he wanted to lay or band stuff. The guys at work had stuff to do. And even though I taught Janie how to give a good right hook, I wasn't about to tell a ten-year-old how horrible it felt to live in a garage surrounded by yard stuff with no hope of leaving any time soon.

I wished emails were like text chains so I could see whether she was typing. But I couldn't, so I refreshed the screen again.

One new email.

From: ThePerfectStranger
To: ADAM

I'll just say thank you one last time because I really am grateful to have someone to talk to. I couldn't exactly tell my mom about my ex. She has enough to worry about already. So, thanks.

When we had that big fight about college, I told him why I needed to stick around here, but he said I was just making excuses because I was scared to go out on my own. That I "wasn't ready to go somewhere where I wasn't constantly saving the day." He even went as far as saying I wanted to be a martyr, but that couldn't be further from the truth.

I never thought I'd be that girl who needed to be with someone. I have a friend like that, and it drives me crazy that she can't be alone, but I guess I get it now. It's nice to know that you have someone in your corner, not just because you've been friends since kindergarten or because you're related. I loved being the girl on his arm when we went out, and I loved holding hands at the movies. But you're right. It wouldn't be the same if he was halfway across the country and I was still here. I'd miss out on all the things I like about having a boyfriend. But my ex is a great guy who's going places. Would I be insane not to see where it led?

ThePerfectStranger

PS-Maybe just...what do you want to do after we graduate? Are you a writer or is this just a hobby?

Why hadn't I suggested she talk to her parents about it? I needed to tuck that in my back pocket for advice to someone else. But for me, going to my parents was laughable. Asking your dad about girl troubles through a glass window was ridiculous. And Mom?

She hadn't really talked much since they took Dad away. At least, not to me. Not that we were really chatty or anything before, but still.

I thought about what Stranger said, about having someone to hold hands with at the movies. It sounded nice when she wrote it like that. But then again, wasn't she writing me because of the heartache and drama that came with all the romance?

I started typing out my response.

From: ADAM
To: ThePerfectStranger

You're welcome. But ignoring the thank yous starting....now.

Sticking around for your family doesn't make you a martyr or mean you have a "savior complex." It means you have your priorities straight. That your world revolves around someone other than yourself. Don't let him make you feel bad for that.

Being alone isn't so bad. I mean, I don't know what you're like, but it really sucks when a friend has a girlfriend because they kind of disappear for a while.

Maybe ask your friends out to a movie. Just don't hold hands. That might be weird.

I can't tell you what to do—the thing about advice columns is that I just help people figure out what they already know. If you're honest with yourself, I think you might already know the answer, deep down. You just have to do some digging.

Adam

PS – I never really thought about what I wanted to do after high school. Just work, I guess. I'm pretty good with cars, but it's not like it's my passion or anything. What about you?

While I waited for ThePerfectStranger's reply, I typed out a few responses to other questions—some of which I had to research. Like what asexual meant. (Basically just not being sexually attracted to other people.) Or what a furry was. (People who took on the personas of animals.)

Another email came through. When the from line didn't say ThePerfectStranger, a weird disappointed feeling swept through my stomach.

I clicked it open and read the message.

From: WAHS Portal [Setting Things Straight]
To: ADAM
Hey Adam,

I don't know if you remember me or not. I wrote a few weeks back about my mom. I just wanted to tell you thanks. Things are still awkward between us, but thanks to you, I was able to have an honest conversation with her. We don't get to choose our parents, you know? They're just people. Thanks for reminding me of that.

Sincerely,
Setting Things Straight

My chest felt tight, and I stared at the screen until it blurred out of focus. "You're welcome."

I'd never felt like this before—needed, not just for money, but for what I actually had to say.

Another message came in from Stranger.

From: ThePerfectStranger
To: ADAM

Dear Adam,

I don't know if I know how I feel about my ex. Maybe I do. Maybe my heart just wants something different from my brain. Have you ever felt like that?

After high school, I'm going to study political science and minor in Spanish. I want to run for office. I think local government is really important, and with the growing Hispanic population, especially in Oklahoma, I also think it's important to be able to communicate with your constituents. That's the plan anyway. Things change. My mom wanted to be a nurse anesthetist. It's kind of like an advanced nursing position. But then she had me. And Dad wanted her to be a stay-at-home mom, so she hardly even got to work as a nurse. Sometimes I wonder if she would have been happier if she'd actually gotten to follow her dreams....

You know, this might sound like a load of bologna, but I think you should try to find what your passion is. What do you like doing in your free time? Is there something you do that just sets your heart on fire? Like you would do it for free if you had to? I think the world's a better place when people do what makes them happy. And you deserve it.

ThePerfectStranger

PS-All the post scripts are getting tiring. Let's just talk. :) If you want.

From: ADAM
To: ThePerfectStranger

It sounds like you're making the decision between what's smart and what you want. Which means what you want isn't a good idea. So are you willing to live with the consequences of making the "right" choice?

Also, if a career in politics fails, you should definitely consider being a motivational speaker. "What sets your heart on fire?" Hopefully nothing—that sounds painful—but I guess this. I didn't think I would, but I actually like writing this column. I should be doing homework now, but I just find myself reading through all of the emails and thinking up ways to reply to everyone. I wish there was more space in the newspaper. But I don't think "advice columnist" is a really secure job title. Doesn't Abby what's-her-name have the corner on that market?

Do you think your mom regrets it? Choosing her family over work? Maybe she's just like you, selfless. And maybe life isn't about chasing dreams at all costs. Maybe it's just about helping others the way you can in the moment.

Signed,
Adam

PS-I agree.

My eyes felt heavy, and I exited out of the email window. I sighed, rolling my neck back and forth. Dreams were nice and all, but someone had to be practical. Not everyone had parents to fall back on if chasing their passion failed. And passion didn't pay the bills.

But maybe I didn't have to be this guy either—the one people dreaded being partnered with in group projects, the one with all the hard edges. Maybe if things were different, I could give advice in real life, not behind the cover of a keyboard. I wasn't sure where to start with all of that, but I had an idea.

I pulled the packet from social studies out of my backpack and started researching campaign plans. I wasn't going to fall into Nora Wilson's expectations of me. Even though I couldn't stand her and that disappointed look, I was going to be the best project partner she ever had.

EIGHT

NORA

ADAM'S NAME flashed in my inbox, and I hurried to click open his message. Adam wasn't like any guy I knew or hung out with. He actually asked questions before giving advice. And he didn't really give advice; he mostly helped me think through my issues. That was probably why everyone had been going crazy over his column. Trey had said that readership had increased since adding the advice column, and he thought they had a better chance than ever at winning a championship at the newspaper contest.

Adding an advice column might have been the best thing I'd suggested as student body president. But if Adam was a senior, I had no idea how someone else would fill his shoes.

I read over his email, and his words hit me harder than ever. *It sounds like you're making the decision between what's smart and what you want. Which means what you want isn't a good idea. So are you willing to live with the consequences of making the "right" choice?*

What were the consequences of going back to Trey? Risking my heart. Having a long-distance boyfriend. Always coming second to academics. But what about the good consequences? Hearing his motivational speeches. Being on the receiving end of kisses that made me forget my name.

Was it worth it?

From: ThePerfectStranger
To: ADAM

Dear Adam,

How do you always ask these questions that hit me right in the heart? I don't think I've ever talked to someone who was so good at cutting straight to the meat of an issue, and you do it wonderfully. Abby doesn't have anything on you. I think you would be an amazing advice columnist. Have you thought about suggesting the column at *The Oklahoman*? They would be lucky to have you.

As for my mom, she never complains. She just does the best she can, even when she needs help. She would do anything for us. Maybe it's just me that would be unhappy in her position. She relies totally on Dad for all of our income, and I guess the millennial in me thinks that's archaic. I would want to work, even if I had children.

I think you have a good point about helping people where you can, but aren't people the most helpful when they genuinely love what they're doing? Like, have you ever been out to eat where the waitress is totally energetic and kind and loves what she's doing? It makes your day so much better than having some grumpy teenager who would rather be anywhere else. I think whatever gives you that feeling is worth it.

What about your parents? Are they the practical kind? What do they think about you writing the column?

ThePerfectStranger

PS-No more postscripts or I'll start thanking you again!

I waited for nearly thirty minutes for him to reply,

but eventually I got too tired to stay up. I set my laptop on my nightstand and fell asleep, still thinking about the consequences of loving Trey and whether it was worth it.

When I walked downstairs the next morning, Dad was sitting on the couch between two of my younger sisters, Esther and Opal, holding Edith on his lap. Spongebob was playing on the TV.

What? Dad was never home on Saturday mornings anymore.

Dad looked over his shoulder at me. "Hey, Nora Bug."

I sleepily walked toward him and pecked his forehead. "Missed you."

He reached up and gave me an awkward, over-theshoulder hug. But I didn't mind. Seeing him once a week on Sundays wasn't enough.

"How was Guymon?" I asked, wanting to know about Dad's latest stop on the campaign trail.

He snorted. "Dry. But don't tell them I said that."

"Our secret." I winked. The smell of bacon hit my nose, and I breathed it in. "I'm gonna see if Mom needs help."

"Going to," he said.

"What?"

"Going to," he said. "'Gonna' is for people who aren't educated at one of the best schools in the state."

I nodded, keeping my face even. "Right. I'm going to help Mom."

"Great. Thanks."

I padded to the kitchen and saw Amie wearing sweats, moisture already gathered at her hairline. She must have gone on her morning run already. That girl was dedicated.

"Morning, honey," Mom said.

I smiled. "Morning. Need any help?"

She lifted a pancake from the griddle and set it on a plate. "Eat this, will you? I need to see someone eat something other than grapefruit."

Amie stuck out her tongue.

My smile grew. "If you insist."

I sat at the breakfast bar beside Amie and ate, enjoying the blend of chocolate chips and blueberries Mom always put in her pancakes.

"I feel like I've hardly gotten to talk to you girls all week," Mom said. "What's new?"

Amie swallowed a bite of grapefruit. "Ms. Twindle said there might be an agent from the New York City Ballet at our next recital."

Both Mom and I looked at her, shocked. New

York City was Amie's dream.

"That's awesome!" I said, rubbing her shoulder.

Mom hugged her. "You're going to do great."

Amie shoved the empty grapefruit rind away from her, looking down. "Yeah."

I could see it in her face. The same worry about what our family would do without her.

"What about you, Nora?" Mom asked.

I shrugged. "The mental health initiative is going really well. I think people had issues with meditation and mindfulness at first, but I think it's really helping."

Amie nodded. "The advice column is incredible. People are raving about it."

My heart warmed at her praise. She wasn't just my sister; she was a freshman at the school who'd benefit from these things years after I graduated. "I think the columnist is something special."

Footsteps sounded behind us, and Mom smiled at Dad balancing Edith on his hip.

"Did you hear that?" Mom asked. "Nora said the advice column is a huge hit."

Dad looked down at a plate of toast Mom had been building and picked up a piece. "Wish advice columns could solve real problems."

I turned my gaze toward my half-eaten pancake, not feeling hungry anymore. Real problems? Adam wrote to people about life and love and parents and rules. And he'd been helping me off the record. Did Dad mean I didn't have real problems?

Amie put a hand on my knee under the breakfast bar, and I met her beautiful wide eyes. She understood. And she was on my side.

My tongue felt thick, and I swallowed. I rubbed my hand on top of hers, then stood up. "I better go get some homework done."

Mom took my plate from me and kissed my forehead. "Love you, hon."

I pulled up one corner of my mouth. "You too."

The first thing I did when I got to my room was check my computer for another email from Adam. No matter what Dad thought of advice columns, it was helping me to have someone to talk to. But Adam hadn't emailed me, so I did the next best thing. I texted London and Grace and asked if they wanted to meet at a coffee shop down the road. They suggested we go to the mall. I said okay.

I went downstairs to doublecheck with Mom and Dad, and they said it was fine as long as I was back by 5:30. Dad wanted us all to go out for supper together.

Within half an hour, I was dressed, out the door, and at the mall. Grace texted me and said they were already in London's favorite store: Victoria's Secret.

With cheeks just as red as the front mannequin's

brassier, I walked into the store, searching for my friends. Personally, I felt embarrassed walking in the place. So much lace I had no idea what to do with. And there were just as many guys as girls in there. Did a guy see a girl walking into the store and wonder what she had under their clothing?

Somewhere between ultra-padded bras and barely-there underwear, I found London and Grace fawning over some sweatpants with PINK written down the side.

When London caught sight of me, she squealed and pulled me into a tight hug.

Despite my morning, I smiled back, then extended my extra arm so Grace could get in on this.

We all hugged for a little while, then pulled apart.

Grace rubbed my arm. "I can't believe you're not out curing cancer or something!"

I rolled my eyes. "Free day. But Dad's taking us out to supper later."

London raised her eyebrows. "He's actually home?"

I pressed my lips together and nodded.

Grace looked confused. "I'm surprised you wanted to come hang out with us then. Did something happen?"

"Long story. I'll tell you later."

London shrugged, seeming appeased. "Okay, so

our mission today, should you choose to accept it, is to find a prom dress."

"What?" I looked between the two of them. "Prom's not 'til April."

Setting down the sweatpants, London said, "And it's already February. Spring always gets crazy for seniors, and I have state cheer coming up, and Grace has church stuff, and you have plenty to do, Madam President. This might be our last chance to prom shop together, and we're taking advantage."

She had a point. Even though it felt like forever in the moment, high school was flying by. It would be the end of the year before we knew it. They would be off to their awesome futures—London cheering at a state school in Kansas and Grace going to West Texas A&M with her friend Fabio—and I'd be...here.

Shaking off the sinking feeling in my core, I looped my arms through both of theirs like old times and led them straight out of Victoria's Secret. We wouldn't be finding anything remotely appropriate in there.

After sorting through racks and racks of gowns, I was starting to wish I'd insisted on the coffee shop. My arms were tired, my hair staticky from pulling dresses on and off, and London showed no signs of slowing down with the constant stream of dresses she sent my and Grace's way.

This latest one was enormous. There had to be at least fifteen layers of tulle under the skirt, and the sleeves were puffy.

"London!" I cried and came out of the dressing room.

Both she and Grace were wearing equally ridiculous poofy gowns. I took them in, London's chest almost spilling out of her dress, petite Grace looking like she was getting swallowed by a taffeta mouse trap. And then I cracked up laughing.

London grinned, showing off a set of fake Halloween teeth, and I laughed even harder.

"What?" she said, crossing her eyes. "Is there thomething in my teef?"

She picked at them. "Spinach mayhapth?"

I clenched at my stomach. "Stop."

She came up closer, baring the teeth in my face. "Help me check, doll fathe."

I fell to the floor in a pile of tulle, still laughing, and they sat on the floor with me. I took their hands in mine. "I love you guys."

London spit her teeth into her hands, curled her lips around her actual teeth, and stuck the plastic ones out to me. "But do you lub me enough to clean my dentures?"

When I finally stopped crying from laughing, I found the dress. Well, Grace found it for me. As we shopped, we didn't talk about boys or breakups or parents, and it was perfect. Like I could escape my life for the first time in a long time. Shopping with the girls had been just what I needed.

I came through the front door to my house with my garment bag over my arms, ready to show Amie my new find, but I stopped and gaped at the living room couch.

Trey was sitting there with my dad, wearing khakis and a navy blazer.

At the sound of the closing door, they both turned their heads toward me.

"Hey, Nora Bug," Dad said.

"Hello?" I looked at Trey. "What are you doing here?"

Dad chuckled uncomfortably. "Is that how you usually greet your boyfriend?"

Oh. Right. "That's not what I meant. Sorry. I just wasn't expecting you."

Dad gripped Trey's shoulder. "I invited him to supper with us." He grinned proudly, like I should be excited.

Trey watched me, looking almost scared. "Is that okay?"

My lips twitched into a smile. "Yeah. Of course." I lifted my arm toward the stairs. "I'm going to get changed."

Dad nodded. "Wear a dress. Probably not that one."

I nodded. "Sure."

I ran up the stairs to change. I couldn't believe Dad had invited Trey without asking me. The last thing I wanted this weekend was to spend time with Trey or share the limited time I had with my dad. I hardly got to see him as it was. And whenever Trey was around, Dad only wanted to talk to him about basketball and the school newspaper. Never mind that Amie was excelling in ballet or that Opal had just gotten her green belt in karate. Or that Esther and Edith missed their dad and just wanted time with him.

I changed into a skirt, blouse, and elbow-length blazer. Then I touched up my curls with a curling iron and went downstairs.

Dad and Trey took me in, but they had totally different expressions on their faces. Where Trey lit up, the crease between Dad's eyebrows deepened.

"You don't have a longer skirt?" Dad asked.

I looked down at the one I was wearing. It came to my fingertips. "Is this not okay?"

He shook his head. "Knee length. Why do I have to keep telling you and Amie this? You're setting a bad example for Opal."

Opal looked up from the couch where she sat in a long skirt and beautiful, jewel-toned shirt.

I sighed. Opal didn't need help. She practically came out of the womb looking like the picture-perfect governor's daughter. On my way up the stairs, I passed a thoroughly disgruntled Amie wearing pants. That wasn't a bad idea.

Finally, we were all dressed, out the door, and squeezed into Mom's minivan. With Trey along, we filled every seat. He and I sat in the middle next to each other. He held my hand under the cover of night, running his thumb back and forth. The touch felt warm, familiar. And it grounded me in the moment.

Dad pulled up to one of his favorite restaurants. It wasn't a fancy place, but it had booster seats for the younger two, plenty of healthy options for Amie, and massive booths so we could all sit together.

The place was loud when we walked in—most of the noise came from a group of guys sitting at a corner booth.

Dad's lips pursed, but he didn't say anything. He was good at making people think he liked them—his number-one rule of politics.

Edith squirmed in Mom's arms, reaching for me, and I let go of Trey's hand so I could hold her. Trey frowned—he wasn't so good at hiding his feelings.

The closer we got to our table, the more I recognized the group in the corner. In between one guy with blue hair and another one with gauges the size of my thumbnail, was my social studies partner: Emerick Turner.

NINE

EMERICK

WOLF'S FRIEND Blue nudged my shoulder. "You know her, Rick? She's hot."

He must have followed my eyes, seen the girl I was watching hold her younger sister, standing next to Mr. "Dog's bitch."

Wolf talked through a mouthful of burger. "That's his social studies partner."

Blue ran his hand through his neon hair. "Wouldn't mind studying her."

Ace, their other band member, shook his head, narrowly avoiding impaling himself on his spiked collar. "Dude, you'd ruin her."

Blue nodded like that was a good thing, and my gut flopped.

I took a bite of my own food, trying to ignore the weird feeling spreading in my chest. Yeah, Nora was a stuck-up, judgmental Barbie doll dating demented-asshole Ken, but these twenty-something-year-old guys had no business checking out a high schooler.

"Okay." Wolf stood up in the booth, and I looked around, waiting for a waitress to come tell him off. He held up his cup of Mountain Dew. "A toast. To the Copperheads." He lifted his cup toward me, and Mountain Dew sloshed over the edges, splattering on the table. "And their roadie." I rolled my eyes. "May our strings be tight, may our girls be hot, and may our music rock forever."

Blue lifted his cup. "Hell yeah!"

Ace banged his forks together, and I laughed, holding up my own half-empty water. Wolf hopped to the ground from the booth and headbanged over an air guitar. "And now, we rock."

We dropped money on the table and jogged out behind him, rushing past Nora's family staring at us exactly the way she had when she found out we'd be partners.

On my way out the door, I almost ran into a couple guys holding microphones and cameras. I glanced back toward Nora's family, and our eyes locked. She looked just as surprised about the cameras as I was.

In the back of Ace's station wagon, sitting between the drum set and guitar cases, my guts twisted even more. Did her family just go out for a photo op? My friends might have been stupid, but at least we could go out just for fun.

It felt like I was cramped up in the trunk forever. Del City wasn't exactly a short drive from where we lived in Warr Acres, a little suburb of Oklahoma City, but eventually we parked behind a grungy joint with a neon sign that spelled Otto's. Except the t's were burnt out, so it just spelled Oo's.

I helped the guys carry in the drum set, and some bartender who barely looked older than me led us to a little stage up front. We set up the drums, guitar stands, and amps, then I went to sit at the bar while I waited for them to do their thing. Blue had a voice like Kurt Cobain, Ace was one of the best drummers I'd ever heard, and Wolf never went anywhere without his guitar. Together, they formed this cool blend between metal and alternative that people ate up.

I asked the bartender for a beer, and he served it up without checking my ID. This was the slow part of the show—before the music really started, but after they needed my help. So I pulled out my phone and went to my email.

One new message from ThePerfectStranger.

The bartender put a beer on the counter, and I took a sip before reading it. Mrs. Arthur had made me advice columnist, for whatever insane reason, but ThePerfectStranger would have been way better at it. She had a way of cutting through all the crap and the excuses. And she was right about people being the worst when they did things they didn't want to.

I thought of Wolf and his part-time job at a local burger joint. He was absolutely miserable as a cook there, but on stage, he looked like he was at home, like he belonged there. And me? Well, I wasn't absolutely sure what I wanted to do. If I was honest with myself, working at Uncle Ken's shop for the rest of my life wasn't it. But what would my family think of me if I became a columnist? Not just one who wrote about politics and things that made a difference, but an advice column. The kind that housewives wrote into about their shitty mothers-in-law and their husbands' drinking problems.

Even as I thought it, I knew minimizing what I did was a load of crap. No matter what anyone said, the column at school mattered. I'd read enough emails to know that people were hurting, and the thank-you email from Setting Things Straight shifted something in me.

From: ADAM
To: ThePerfectStranger

Hey Stranger,

I totally get what you mean about people being in the wrong job. I have a friend who works in fast food, but he should totally give that up. Honestly, it's not hard to slap a burger together, but he still gets complaints. He's way better doing what he loves. Which happens to be nearly as impractical as writing an advice column. But at least he can play at weddings and quinceneras and stuff. It's not like I can sit on a street corner asking people to tell me about their problems. But that's a good idea about *The Oklahoman*. Maybe I'll check them out.

About my parents...It's complicated. My mom's very practical, but Dad's always been into get-rich-quick schemes. (It never works out, for the record.) My dad doesn't know I'm writing the column, but I don't think Mom's too concerned about it either way. They mostly just let me do my thing and hope I stay out of trouble. Which I do. Most of the time. ;)

So, I was out with my friends tonight, and I thought of you. About how people have different expectations of you just because of who you are. There are people out there who live lives so different from mine, and I wonder what they think when they see me. I know I shouldn't care about what other people think, but sometimes it gets to me. Sometimes, I just want to know what it would feel like to be someone else for a day.

But that's enough existential stuff for now. Tell me about you. Something no one else knows.

Signed,
Adam

PS-Okay. ;)

I set my phone down and took another drink from the beer. It wasn't the greatest, but it was wet and warmed my throat.

The guys started with their first song, and since the crowd was still thin, they didn't get too much applause. But they kept playing, looking like the stage was their own world.

I refreshed my email screen and grinned to see ThePerfectStranger had replied.

From: ThePerfectStranger

To: ADAM

Dear Adam,

What you've done with the advice column is nothing short of amazing. Don't sell yourself short. And do check out *The Oklahoman*. And other newspapers too.

Something no one else knows about me? I write to this guy I've never met in person, and I look forward to his messages more than I'd like to admit.

It's funny that you thought about me tonight, because I thought about you too. I don't know what people think when they see you, but I know what they think about me. They think I'm just another little Pollyanna with a perfect life, perfect parents, perfect siblings, and the perfect clothes. My parents make sure of that, though. My dad won't let me leave the house unless I'm dressed perfectly. And my ex even comments on stuff like that sometimes. Like if my fingernail polish is chipped, he'll point it out. The pressure on top of everything else is crushing me, but I don't know how to tell them I'm tired of it without just sounding like a pathetic, whiney baby.

If you could start fresh, how would you want people to see you?

ThePerfectStranger

PS-Okay, I'm stopping this postscript now.

If I was being honest, I looked forward to her messages more than work or school or anything else. And it made me feel a little less pathetic that she felt the same way. Right away, I hovered my thumbs over the keyboard, but I couldn't find an answer to her question. *How would you want people to see you?*

"How are you doing tonight, Del City?" Blue asked into the mic. It was so loud now I could feel the vibrations in my chest.

People on the little dance floor in front of the stage clapped and cheered.

"Alright, alright, alright," Blue said. "My name's Blue, this is Ace, and this is Wolf, and we are the Copperheads."

More cheers.

Wolf began strumming a melody on his guitar.

"You've all heard of 'Copperhead Road,' right?" Blue said.

More cheers.

Blue chuckled low in his throat. "Well, we have our own version. Same moves, different beat."

Wolf went heavier on the guitar, Ace began banging on the drums, and Ace said, "Rick, why don't you get out here and show them the moves?"

A grin split my face, and I gave a chin nod to the guys. This was my favorite part of going to their shows. But first? I downed my beer.

"'Atta boy," Blue said.

I stepped to the front of the crowd and began the dance. The rock 'n' roll version of "Copperhead Road" was way better, in my opinion. I let the music take over, not worrying about what the people behind me thought of my moves or how I looked as I shimmied side to side. I just danced, and at the end, electric energy filled my veins.

A guy next to me stuck his hand up for a high five, and I returned it, grinning.

"Hey," he yelled in my ear. "I want you to meet my girl's friend."

The girl next to him was hot, busty with thick black eyeliner around her eyes, but then her friend stepped forward. She had on a tube top showing off her pierced navel and deep cleavage with lips tattooed right where her breasts swelled out of her shirt. Her hair brushed against her shoulders, and I wanted to push it back, see the length of her collarbone.

The guy clapped my back. "Have fun."

The girl stepped forward, putting her mouth next to my ear. "Heya, handsome. What's your name?"

I swallowed. "Rick."

She stepped back and grinned. "Lacey. But you can call me yours."

Damn, she was laying it on thick. And the way her lips moved around her words? Again, damn.

"Wanna dance?" I asked before I knew what I was saying.

She nodded. And we danced to the next song, doing some strange mix between grinding and fast dancing and slow dancing. It totally wouldn't have gone over well at a school dance.

Lacey-call-me-yours didn't seem to mind. She just kept pouting at me with those kiss-me lips and swaying her body in a way that made me hope the integrity of her tube top wouldn't last long.

After the song, she took my hand and put it over her shoulder so she could lead me outside. Like a puppy on the world's sexiest leash, I followed.

Outside the bar, she leaned against a wall and propped her foot up, making her skirt ride up even further. From deep in her cleavage, she pulled out a pack of cigarettes and offered me one.

I shook my head and leaned against the wall.

A sexy smirk on her lips, she took it out for herself and lit it with a cleavage-lighter. Her full lips moved around the butt of the cigarette and left a line of lipstick. White smoke poured through her nose.

She watched me watching her and smiled. "You're cute."

I swallowed. "You're hot."

Her head tipped forward, spilling her hair over her face, and she giggled.

Why didn't I date? Girls were nice—they had the best laughs, and they smelled a hell of a lot better than Wolf. Plus, those lips. Those curves. I bit down on my bottom lip, thinking of all the things I'd been missing out on.

She peeked around her hair and looked up at me, batting her long eyelashes. "Why don't we get out of here?"

TEN

NORA

"TREY, YOU DON'T GET IT," I said, dropping onto my bed.

He sat in my desk chair, his tie hanging loose around his neck. "I guess I don't. What's the deal? If having the media there helped your dad's chances at winning governor, wasn't it worth it?"

My chest ached. He really didn't get it. "It's not about whether it was worth it or not. It's about the fact that since this whole campaign started, I've hardly seen my dad. Edith and Esther asked for me and Mom to tuck them in, not Dad. And then we have him home for the first Saturday night in months, and he takes us out, invites you,"—I ignored Trey's hurt look—"and then I learn it was all a publicity stunt to show how he's the perfect 'family man.'" I used quote fingers.

"He *is* a family man," Trey said. "You know he's running for governor to make Oklahoma a better place to live for you and your sisters. And that means you'll have to sacrifice for a little while. Honestly, you're being a little selfish."

I raised my eyebrows. Trey talking about sacrifice, calling *me* selfish? That was rich.

My phone beeped on the edge of my dresser.

Trey stood up to get it, but I hurried to reach it before he could.

His eyebrows came together. "Who's that from?"

I held the phone behind my back. "No one."

A few knocks sounded on my door, and it came open.

Trey's face automatically shifted from accusatory to charming, dimpled smile and all.

Mom peeked her head in. "You know the rule. Open doors." But she said it with a smile, like she was proud our clothes were securely in place and we didn't have our tongues down each other's throats.

"Sorry, Mrs. Wilson," Trey said.

She nodded. "That's alright. It is getting late though."

"You're right." Trey stood up and hooked his blazer over his shoulder with his finger. "I better get home." He turned to me. "Talk to you at church tomorrow?"

Translation: I'll interrogate you at church tomorrow.

"Goodnight," I said.

Trey left, but Mom stayed in the doorway. "Everything okay, honey?"

My eyes stung, and I stared at the ceiling. "I'm fine."

She leaned against the door frame, probably waiting for me to fall apart so she could help hold me together. But that wasn't my life. My family depended on me to be the perfect daughter, to look good in photo shoots and be a star student and drive my sisters place to place. Breaking down didn't fit into that facade.

I took in a deep breath and smiled at her. "That monte cristo was really good, huh?"

"It was good." Her smile softened, and she came closer, kissing me on the forehead. "Goodnight, honey. Your dad and I are so proud of you."

I tugged my lips back and fought tears until she left and shut the door behind her. Then they spilled down my face. Dad wasn't proud of me. No matter how hard I tried, it was never good enough.

After slipping out of my future-governor-approved pantsuit, I went to bed, bringing my phone with me, and slid under the covers. Using the edge of my quilt, I wiped at my eyes so I'd be able to see Adam's message.

From: ADAM
To: The Perfect Stranger
Hey Stranger,

I've never thought about how I'd want people to see me, just how I didn't want them to see me. But now that I think about it, I want them to see me as a good, honest guy. The kind you can depend on if you have a flat tire in the middle of the night or one who would take a drunk girl home and set some Gatorade and aspirin by the bed for when she wakes up in the morning. And even though that's the kind of person I am, it's not like anyone believes that.

And this guy you're writing to? He's lucky as hell. He looks forward to your messages, too, even though you say thank you way too much and are way too smart and nice. You make him want to be a better guy, just so he doesn't keep getting shown up. ;)

So, did you have a good night at least?

Signed,

Adam

PS-Can't stop, won't stop the PS.

A smile touched my lips. The first one since I read his last email. What would it be like to meet Adam in person? Would he be fun? Serious? Would we be able to talk like this without the cover of pen names and computer screens? I didn't know. All I knew was that I wanted to write him back.

From: ThePerfectStranger
To: ADAM
Dear Adam,

How could people not see you that way? You write an advice column for crying out loud! Maybe one of the best advice columns I've ever read. That has to translate into your everyday life. I don't know if we've ever met, but I have to believe that if I saw you, I'd be able to tell how kind you are.

And I'm happy you like hearing from me too. Otherwise that would be kind of awkward. But really, is there such a thing as too smart and too kind? (Asking for a friend.)

My night? It was a disaster. Honestly. There was this huge jungle at our family dinner—more than the normal kind with so many siblings. And my ex came. Can you believe this? He actually told me I was being selfish for wanting my dad to be around and spend more time with us. And the worst part? I actually believed him for a second.

ThePerfectStranger

PS-You're the worst. Thank you. ;)

Within a few minutes, my phone chimed again, and instead of reading on the tiny screen, I pulled out my laptop.

From: ADAM
To: ThePerfectStranger
Hey Stranger,

You might be surprised how people see me. At the risk of sounding like a cliché, looks can be deceiving. But it makes me feel better that you wouldn't judge me.

Let your friend know there isn't such a thing. I like it. Really.

And I'm sorry about your family dinner not going well. If it makes you feel any better, I can't remember the last time I sat down to eat supper with both of my parents around. Sometimes I eat with my uncle's family, though, and that's always a survival-of-the-fittest type event. Imagine three kids under ten fighting for fish sticks and you'll have a general idea of what it's like.

I'm sorry, but your ex was totally out of bounds for calling you selfish. There's not a lot of black and white in the world, but this is one of them: you are not selfish. Not even close.
But it's getting late. We should both get some sleep. Talk to you tomorrow?

Signed,
Adam

My eyelids felt heavy, but I wrote him back.

From: The Perfect Stranger
To: ADAM
Dear Adam,

Fighting over fish sticks. It sounds like you were at my house. And thank you for being so nice to me. I'm really happy I decided to email you.

Talk to you tomorrow.

ThePerfectStranger

In the morning, Mom woke me up for church, and it was a mad dash to get myself and all of my siblings ready, even with Dad around. He had work to do since he had to drive across the state in the evening for more campaigning.

When we were all dressed to Dad's standards, we piled into the van and drove to St. Charles for Mass. There weren't a ton of Catholics in Oklahoma, but we had a good church family of people from all over the world. But that morning, I wished my parents were the type of Catholics who would just get in and get out.

Mom and Dad always stayed around to talk while the younger kids played in the little gym attached to the church. They sat down with some friends at a table in the gym, and I sat with them. Which, unfortunately, meant Trey had ample time to find me.

He came to stand beside my seat. "Hey, Nora."

I glanced up at him. How hadn't I noticed he had a little gap between his two front teeth? Now, as he smiled at me, it seemed like that little space was all I could see.

"Want to walk around?" he asked.

I glanced back at Mom. "I'm keeping an eye on my sisters."

Mom rested her hand on my forearm. "Go ahead, honey. I've got it."

Thanks, Mom.

I stood up and followed Trey to the walking path around the inside of the gym.

When we got out of earshot of the other adults and children playing tag, he said, "Nora, have you been thinking about us?"

I nodded. I had a hard time thinking of anything else.

His hand tightened around my waist. "And?"

Tired of his grip, of the pressure, I stepped back.

There wasn't a good way to say this. "Look, Trey. I don't think we're well-suited for each other."

He rubbed his hand over his smooth jaw. "'Well-suited'?"

I folded my arms across my stomach and let him process.

His eyes penetrated me, boring into mine. "Are you serious? We're the 'it' couple."

"Do you hear yourself?" I raised my eyebrows. "This isn't about me; it never has been. It's just been about stoking your ego." I could see that more clearly than ever now.

Trey came a step closer. "You're doing this here?"

"What?" Then realization hit. "You just talked to me at church because you didn't want me to be able to say no and make a scene."

My mom called from across the gym. "Nora!"

I looked over my shoulder.

"Ready to go?" she asked.

"Yeah." I called and made sure to say a quick thank-you prayer for my mom's intervention.

Trey's lips pressed together. "This isn't over."

I started toward Mom, ignoring Trey. He was right. There wasn't a word for how over we were.

High from the giddiness of finally making a decision about Trey, I emailed Adam on the ride home.

From: ThePerfectStranger
To: ADAM

Dear Adam,

I did it! I ended things for good with my ex. So, I know you don't like thank-yous, but thank you. I never would have been able to do it without you. Email me when you have time. I have something crazy to ask you. :)

Stranger

I signed the email as Stranger, but maybe I wouldn't be for long.

ELEVEN
EMERICK

STAYING out all night was stupid. Especially since I went straight from hanging out with Wolf, Blue, and Ace to my Sunday morning shift at the shop. I used a napkin to rub my eyes, then poured even more tar-black coffee into my travel mug. Technically, the stuff was supposed to be for waiting customers, but they'd be waiting a long time if I fell asleep.

Even though we'd had fun after the guys and I dropped Lacey off at her apartment, I was seriously regretting it. I still had a ton of homework to do, and I needed to get a jump on the column for my Thursday deadline.

On my way back to the garage, I pulled out my phone to check my emails. When I read the one from ThePerfectStranger, my heart both soared and sank. She wanted to meet me. I just knew it. How could I tell her I couldn't? Not just because I wouldn't be what she was expecting, but because I'd literally fail my senior year if my identity got revealed.

Shouts reached my ears, but not soon enough. My foot hit a slick spot on the ground, slid out from under me, and slammed into a jack holding up the back end of a compact car. Then pain. Like I'd never felt before.

Blinding white lights.

Shouting.

Grunting.

Screaming. That came from me.

And then I looked down at my leg and saw the car frame had sliced all the way through my jeans, down to my broken bone.

I leaned over and threw up. But then I couldn't feel anything, just saw it all happening like it was someone else's body getting loaded onto a stretcher, riding in the ambulance, being rushed through the emergency entrance to the hospital, being told I'd have to go into surgery immediately if I had any hope of keeping my leg from the knee down.

And then blackness.

I blinked my eyes open to a white room and flashing monitors. To dull, throbbing pain below my knee. To my mom and uncle sitting with me.

Uncle Ken sat in the corner, flipping through a magazine. Mom had her chin resting on her folded hands. She was still wearing her scrubs, and her eyes looked purple underneath.

"Mom?" I grunted.

Mom's tired eyes jerked up to me. "Emerick?" She stood up and crushed me in a hug. Wires be damned. "Oh my god, baby." She pulled back, her hands running over my chest, my cheeks. "How do you feel?"

Uncle Ken came to stand beside her, taking me in.

"Like you look." I tried to chuckle but started coughing instead.

Tears sprang to her eyes. "You had me worried sick."

My uncle nodded, the crease between his eyes more pronounced than I'd ever seen it.

I blinked. "What...what happened?" My lower half was covered with blankets. "What about the surgery?"

They looked at each other.

Uncle Ken stepped forward. "Son, you shattered the two bones in your calf. They kept your leg, but you're gonna need another surgery in a couple months. It'll be a long time before you're walking on it again, and you might never walk without a limp."

Me? Injured? I looked down at the blankets

covering my leg. How could that be true? I'd never even sprained an ankle or needed stitches on the job.

"How am I supposed to work?" I asked.

Uncle Ken put a hand on my shoulder. "You just worry about getting better. We can talk about that later."

I wanted to stand up and argue, to fight. I propped myself up on my elbows, but Uncle Ken pushed me back down. "You need to calm down, son."

"No," I spat. "I need to work. We've got bills to pay. Ma, you can't work twenty-four hours a day."

Mom closed her eyes and shook her head. "Baby, you leave that to me."

"How you gonna pay Dad's credit card bills, huh? You wanna be on Ken's couch forever?"

Uncle Ken squeezed my shoulder, probably trying to relax me, but it just pissed me off. What were they thinking? That some unicorn was going to fly over and shit money on us?

"I'll be at work Monday," I told Ken.

"That might be a little hard since they want to keep you here for a week," Ken said.

"I'll be at work Monday," I repeated.

Mom ran her hand over my hair and kissed my forehead. "I love you, baby. You just gotta let go and let God."

Mom was always saying shit like that when we actually had time to talk, but I didn't know how. Her husband was in the pen. Her son had to work a full-time job on top of school to pay off debts. She was working two jobs and living with her brother. This was rock bottom. This was what "letting go and letting God" looked like.

"Listen," Uncle Ken said, his voice taking on that hard, no-arguments, paternal tone I rarely heard from my own dad. "This is why we have insurance. We're gonna get a worker's comp case going. You'll have your hospital bills paid for, maybe even have some extra wages while you're recovering. Will you give me a week to work it out and just focus on getting better during that time?"

My eyes stung as the weight of it all hit me. Shattered bones. Another surgery. Never walking without a limp. Worker's comp.

With Mom and Ken on either side, I couldn't get privacy, so I just sniffed and wiped at my face with the hand that wasn't attached to an IV.

Uncle Ken squeezed my shoulder again. "Love you, son. Linda and Janie are worried sick. Let me go get them."

Mom looked at Ken. "What about the boys?"

He chuckled. "You know little kids. They were

just happy that supper came out of a vending machine."

They both left, giving me a second to myself. I needed it, because I didn't want Janie to walk in and see me falling apart.

Aunt Linda came into the room first, but Janie was close behind, clinging to her mother's hand and peeking around behind her back, even though she was getting closer and closer to Linda's height every day.

I smiled at her, and she dropped her mom's hand and ran to the bed. She came to a stop at the railing, her eyes wide as Uncle Ken's waistline.

"Hey, Janie," I rasped.

Her little lips trembled, and water filled her eyes.

"Hey, hey, hey," I said, fighting to make my voice sound closer to normal. "I'm okay."

Being careful of the wires, she launched through the gap in the railing and squeezed me, sobbing into my chest.

I wrapped my arms around her, rubbing her back. Having her there was just what I needed to fall apart. We cried together for who knows how long, with Linda stroking her back and my shoulder.

Eventually our sobs subsided, and she pulled back to look at me. She used her thumb to wipe away some tears from my cheek. "I'm glad you're alive."

I snorted. "Me too. Here." I scooted over as best I could with a giant cast around my leg. "Come sit with me. I need someone to hog the remote."

A smile lit up her still-damp face. "I can watch anything?"

"Anything."

"Even Disney Channel?"

I suppressed a groan. "Even that. Come on." I patted the empty space, and she came around to my side.

Aunt Linda sat with us for a while, but eventually she left, and it was just Janie and me watching TV. The show wasn't half bad, other than the kids were brats and the parents were idiots. But slowly, I drifted into sleep, snuggled next to the little girl who had my back, no matter what.

Someone knocking on the door woke Janie and me up, and I looked up to see Wolf and his bandmates walking into the room. Wolf's face was paler than usual, and that was saying something.

"Hey, Janie?" I said.

She rubbed at her eyes. "Yeah?"

"You remember how to give a right hook?"

Everyone looked at me confused, but Janie nodded.

"If Wolf keeps looking at me like that, I want you to go practice on him."

They let out some nervous laughter, but it was enough to break the ice.

Wolf lifted up my backpack, which he had slung around his shoulder. "Your mom asked if we could stop by the house and get your stuff. Thought you might get bored."

I gave him a half smile. "What? In a ritzy place like this?" I nudged Janie. "With Disney Channel on?"

Linda stepped from behind Blue, giving his wild hair the side-eye. "Come on, Janie. We better get you home. You have school tomorrow."

She pouted, but I told her I'd see her after school, and she eventually left with her mom.

The guys stayed to talk for a little while, but soon a doctor came in with Mom and Uncle Ken and there were too many people around, so the guys left.

The doctor repeated all the things Mom and Uncle Ken had said earlier, but he had pictures to prove his point. I barely recognized the bones in my leg, with little pieces around and a giant rod he said they had to put in to "facilitate healing."

At this point, I was numb to it all. I'd had my cry, I'd heard the news. Now it was just a matter of figuring out how in the hell to get back to work.

The doctor lowered my file. "You're lucky to be alive, Emerick. Just another foot, and you would have hit your femoral artery and bled out before the ambulance could even get there."

That hit me. Hard. So hard, I was still thinking about it after Mom and Ken left to get some sleep, after the nurse came and poked and prodded me, after I massacred the bedpan.

I stared at the white ceiling tiles thinking about that. I could have been dead right now, and I would have spent my whole life doing shit other people wanted me to do. Working myself to death to make up for my dad's mistakes. Never thinking about what I wanted or what was possible. I wasn't going to be the guy who wakes up at forty or fifty hating my job and wondering where my life went.

I set my laptop on my lap and started looking up newspaper jobs. I typed up a resume and cover letter using examples from the Internet. And then I did the stupidest thing of all: I applied for an unpaid internship at *The Oklahoman*.

I wanted to email ThePerfectStranger about my injury, but that would be too close to real. I mean, how many kids in school could shatter their leg on the same weekend? Probably none. Still, after the kind of day I had, I wanted to talk to her.

I had to read the email she sent me twice to take it all in.

She officially broke it off with her ex!

The amount of joy that swept through me, even after all the bad news I'd had that day, seemed unreal, but my good feelings quickly evaporated.

Why was I grinning like a damn fool? Because some girl I would never be able to meet in person—at least not until the end of the year—broke up with her boyfriend. And not just any boyfriend. She'd referred to them as the "it couple." That meant she wasn't just some average girl at WAHS. She was an "it" girl, and "it" girls didn't go out with shit guys like me. Nora was proof of that. Not that I wanted to date her. But she wouldn't even look at me.

Thoroughly deflated, I replied to Stranger's email, ignoring the fact that she'd wanted to ask me a question. Meeting her could never end well.

From: ADAM
To: ThePerfectStranger
Hey Stranger,

Congratulations. How does it feel now that the decision's behind you?

Signed,
Adam

After that, I checked the time. It was only half past ten.

I closed my laptop and sent Nora a text.

TWELVE
NORA

USUALLY, I was falling into bed by now, but my mind wouldn't stop running. I should have been distracted by the craziness that had passed between Trey and me. But no, the thing that really kept me up was Adam and his emails, wondering if I'd seen him, if I knew him already.

Had this amazing guy been right under my nose and I'd been too blind to see it?

My phone went off, and within seconds, I had his email opened, scanning over it. He'd only written a few sentences, and I was smiling like an idiot. How could I be falling for some guy I didn't even know when Trey, basketball captain, senior class vice president, and editor of the *WAHS Ledger*, was practically begging me to be his girlfriend?

I typed out a quick response and hit send before I could talk myself out of it.

My phone went off almost immediately, and disappointment swept through me. It was too soon for it to be a reply from Adam. Sighing, I opened the text.

Emerick: Hey, I'm sorry, but I had a little accident. I'm going to be at the hospital for the week, but I've been working on our project. Want to come by after school to work on it?

Great. Just what I needed. Another thing to take care of outside of school. But then I felt guilty for thinking that. It must have been a pretty bad accident if he was in the hospital.

Nora: I hope everything's okay. I can't do after school, but maybe I could come by early on Tuesday?

Three dots popped up on the screen, and I waited.

Emerick: That's fine. I'm at St. Anthony's. Room 622.

Nora: I'll be by at 6:30. Is that too early?

Emerick: It's fine. See you then.

I shut down my phone and closed my eyes, feeling a little less shameful. If it had been that bad, he wouldn't be texting me about school at 10:30 p.m. Actually, from what I knew about him, this was probably his first time thinking about homework outside of school. Good for him.

In the morning, our house was crazy, as usual. I helped pack lunches while Amie cooked breakfast and Mom got the younger three ready.

Amie and I left first, then Mom would load the other three in her van and take off to bring Opal to middle school. We'd gotten into a routine without having Dad around. It wasn't perfect, but it worked.

The second Amie and I got to school, London and Grace assaulted me with questions, London at the forefront.

"Did you really break up with Trey?" she asked.

Grace looked hurt. "Why didn't you tell us?"

London nodded. "And why did you dump him?"

I lifted my hands, trying to calm the storm. "Whoa, whoa, whoa." I looked around the front hallway to the school, at all the kids milling around who could overhear us. "Come on." I led them to homeroom, and we stood in the corner of the classroom.

"Okay," I whispered. "I broke up with Trey. I didn't tell you because I just decided to do it yesterday. And actually, he broke up with me before Christmas break."

London's mouth fell slack. "He broke up with you?"

I closed my eyes and nodded, trying to forget how miserable I'd been over break. "He basically said that I was wasting my future by going to OU and he didn't want a girlfriend back home to tie him down. But then he asked me to take him back pretty shortly after school started back up. And I said I'd think about it."

Grace's eyes were wide. "That must have been so hard. You know you could have talked to us about it, right?"

My cheeks burned. They were right. Instead, I'd been an idiot and emailed the school's advice columnist. "I was embarrassed about it all."

London nudged my shoulder. "You were there whenever I bled through my pants and Tony Billinger asked if I'd sat on chocolate!"

Grace laughed. "And when I beat up that guy with Fabio's light-up Pokémon shoes."

"That wasn't so embarrassing," I argued. "You were standing up for your friend."

She rolled her eyes. "That's not the point."

"Exactly." London nodded. "The point is, it's the three of us, together. Always has been and always will be."

I smiled and hugged them.

"No more secrets?" London asked.

I nodded, but for whatever reason, I couldn't

bring myself to tell them about Adam. Not yet. Not until I knew how he'd reply to my question.

Classes throughout the day went as usual, except people kept giving me strange looks. Apparently, Trey had publicly changed his relationship status to "single" where I had just hidden mine.

On my way to American Government, I passed him in the hallway with a girl on either side of him. He didn't seem too torn up.

In class, Mr. Roberts stood at the front, holding up two stacks of colored paper. "I have great news. First, we have an official date set for the debates. In addition to the student body, parents are welcome to come. Second,"—he held up the green stack of papers —"we have gotten approval for a trip to the state capitol! We have a fun event planned for the day, but you will need permission from your parents to go."

He passed the papers down the row, and I read over the field trip information. We'd be doing a scavenger hunt with our partner in the capitol building. Maybe I'd actually get to see Dad during the day.

After he gave our class instructions for today's assignment, he came and knelt by my desk. "So, I'm not sure if you heard, but Emerick was in a bad work accident. He won't be in class for a week. Maybe longer if the doctors don't clear him."

I nodded. "He texted me last night."

Mr. Roberts looked just as surprised as I had felt the night before. "So you've got something worked out between the two of you?"

I nodded, and curiosity got the best of me. "Do you know what happened?"

He shook his head, then searched around the classroom until his gaze fell in the general direction of Emerick's friend. "Frederick, come here, will you?"

The guy looked exhausted and pissed. "It's Wolf," he muttered.

Our teacher sighed. "Just come here." When Wolf got close enough, Mr. Roberts asked, "Do you know what happened to Emerick? Is he recovering well?"

Wolf winced. He looked...guilty. "A car fell on him at the shop where he works. Basically shattered his leg. He's lucky to be alive, man."

My hand covered my mouth. I felt just as disgusting as the gum stuck under my desk. How could I have been so callous before? "Is he okay?"

Wolf shrugged. "He was pretty bummed he couldn't get back to work."

Mr. Roberts's eyes widened. "He wanted to go back to work?"

Wolf's eyes met mine, then turned to the floor. "I don't think he had a choice."

Looking disturbed, Mr. Roberts straightened. "Thanks Fred—er—Wolf. Please give him my best."

Wolf hung his head in a nod, then walked back to his partner. And I sat there by myself, wishing for the first time that Emerick was sitting in the empty desk next to mine.

After school and during my shift at city hall, the same person swirled in my thoughts: Emerick. I couldn't imagine how painful that must have been to have an actual car fall on his leg. And how did they get it off? Was he going to keep his leg? Would he need surgery? Would he be able to keep working?

Wolf's words hung in my mind. *I don't think he had a choice.*

It never crossed my mind that Emerick was ditching school to work and make money for someone other than himself. Did he have family members depending on him? How would his injury affect them? Affect him?

The more I thought about it, the more upset I felt. So I stopped thinking about it. At least, I tried.

After the longest shift ever, I was finally able to pick up Amie and head home. On the way inside, Amie opened the mailbox and sorted through the letters.

"This one's for you," she said.

I took in the packet and the OU logo in the corner. I'd already gotten my acceptance letter, but I ripped it open and scanned the note.

My mouth fell open.

"What is it?" Amie asked, her hand on the door handle.

"I just got a Presidential Scholarship—a full ride!"

She dropped her hand from the door handle and screamed, jumping up and down. "Oh my gosh! That's awesome!"

I jumped with her. "You're next! Just wait, you'll get the call from New York."

She wrapped her arm around my shoulder. "Girl, we've got to celebrate you! You have to call Dad! He'll be so excited."

We went inside and told Mom the good news. She actually woke up all the girls so we could eat ice cream at the breakfast bar, and while she was cleaning up, I FaceTimed Dad.

It rang for a really long time before he came into view. I noted the hotel curtains behind him, his dress shirt unbuttoned with his tie loose around his neck.

"Hey, Nora Bug," he said. "What are you doing up so late?"

I tried to ignore the disappointed look in his eyes and held up the letter. "I got a Presidential Scholarship from OU!"

Dad smiled. "Good job, kiddo."

"Thanks, I mean, I was hoping I'd get it, but I just didn't—"

"Nora?" He set the phone down so I had a great view of the popcorn ceiling. "I'm sorry, but I have to get going soon. I have a private meeting set up with some potential donors. I just came back to the room to freshen up." His face came back into view, his tie back in place.

My chest squeezed, but I put on a smile and nodded. "That's fine. I'll talk to you later. Love—"

"See ya, love you," he said and hung up.

Amie rubbed my shoulder. "I'm sor—"

I shook my head and stepped back. "It's okay. I better get to bed. Goodnight."

Instead of emailing Adam like I usually did before bed, I sent Emerick a text saying I'd see him in the morning and tried to fall asleep.

THIRTEEN

EMERICK

AT HALF PAST SIX, Nora came into my room. She walked closer to me, her big doll eyes obviously taking in my elevated leg.

"How—What—" she frowned. "Are you okay?"

I pushed the button that lifted my bed to a good sitting position. "Been better."

Her lips pulled even further down, putting lines in her usually smooth skin. "Are you in pain?"

I shrugged. "Yeah, but medication helps. I held out for this though—didn't want you to see me all loopy."

Her eyes widened. "Don't skip your medicine for me. If you need it, take it."

My lips spread into a smile as I took her in.

Her frown turned to something else. Confusion. "What?"

"Is Nora Wilson actually concerned about little ol' me?"

She sighed and rolled her eyes. "Don't let it go to your head." She sat down in the seat next to my bed and pulled a binder labeled *AMERICAN GOVERN-MENT* from her backpack. "Did you hear about the field trip?"

"Yeah, my ma brought a bunch of homework by yesterday."

She nodded, her eyes flitting from my leg to my face. "Well, what did you think about it?"

"I—" A girl a few years younger than us walked in. She looked almost exactly like Nora, but her face was rounder.

Nora followed my eyes. "Opal, what are you doing here?"

The girl leaned against the wall like she was trying to fade into it. "I was wondering if you had a quarter? I'm a little short for the vending machine."

Nora kept her gaze away from me as she dug in her purse and eventually pulled out a quarter. "Here you go."

The girl held the quarter in her palm. "Sorry," she said, then hurried out.

Nora immediately launched into this story about her mom coming down with something and having to drive both her sisters to school. "I'm sorry. I told them to hang out in the waiting room until we were done."

Nora Wilson having to worry about someone other than herself? Doing something not just because it would look good on a college app? That didn't exactly reconcile with the girl who gave me a snotty look the first day we were announced partners.

"It's okay," I said. "Anyway, I think the trip sounds fine. You probably know your way around the capitol."

She nodded.

"Cool. So..." I checked my binder. "Our first assignment is to describe our ideal voter. I was thinking we should aim more toward the underclassmen. Like the freshmen who are still figuring things out."

Her lips quirked up like she liked the idea but didn't want to give me too much credit. "That could work. Get to them while they're still vulnerable."

"Whoa." I lifted up my hands, and her eyes went to my IV. "I didn't say that. I just meant, they're probably the people who would benefit most from whatever stance we take. You know, since they'll be here longer. And there are more of them."

Now she set a bashful smile on me, and damn, it was cute. How could a girl be such a snot and still look like a total babe?

I caught myself wishing more girls would be like ThePerfectStranger, honest and open and down-to-earth. Her personality with Nora's looks? She'd be a knockout.

But Nora started talking, so I paid attention. She helped divide up the assignment, then packed up her bag and stood to leave.

At the door, she hesitated and looked back. "I'm really sorry you were injured. And I'm glad you're okay."

"I'm not," I said. "But I will be." And I hoped that was true.

Her lips twitched up but fell again, and she turned to leave.

The second she was out the door, I pressed the call button and asked for pain medicine. Two more minutes with Nora, and I would have screamed. But when I said I wanted to be the best partner she'd ever had, I meant it. Being all doped up on Oxy didn't exactly line up with that plan.

The nurse brought the pill, and I slept for a couple of hours before pulling out my computer to check my emails. I hoped to hear from *The Oklahoman* and ThePerfectStranger. But I only had one from ThePerfectStranger.

I clicked it open and read the message. I had to read it twice.

From: ThePerfectStranger
To: ADAM

Dear Adam,

I know this is going to sound crazy, but what if we met in real life? I want to see the person who's been writing me all this time.

ThePerfectStranger

I scrubbed my hand over my face, down over the stubble on my jaw. Shit.

She wanted to meet me. In person.

The problem? I wanted to meet her too.

Well, that wasn't the only problem. Actually, I'd probably need all my fingers and toes to count out all the reasons it wouldn't work. Problem number one, if I revealed my identity to anyone before graduation, I could kiss my high school diploma goodbye. Mrs. Arthur said so herself. Also, ThePerfectStranger was...perfect. Or, at least, that's what she was to everyone else, which meant she probably had a nice family, lived in a decent house. I couldn't exactly ask a girl like that to come hang out on my garage futon and make out between a lawnmower and a bag of fertilizer. And what would she say when she knew my dad was a convicted felon? Huh?

No, I couldn't meet her. Even if I wanted to. Even if she was the one person who knew me better than anyone else, including Wolf.

I had to retype the message three times, but I finally came up with something. The truth.

From: ADAM
To: ThePerfectStranger
Hey Stranger,

I'd love to meet you. But I don't know if I can or if we should. Hearing from you has been the best. Really. But could something like this actually exist in real life? When you can see me for who I really am? Maybe a relationship like this needs to stay on-screen, before it can get messy and I can screw it up.

Signed,
Adam

She didn't respond until late that evening, but I got it.

From: ThePerfectStranger
To: ADAM

Dear Adam,

I've already seen who you really are. You're kind, understanding, thoughtful, caring. Seeing you in person won't change that. But I won't push you. Just know that whenever you're ready, I'm ready. And I hope you'll be ready soon.

ThePerfectStranger

The rest of the week passed like that—working on homework with Nora in the morning, making up assignments during the day, working on the advice column after school hours, and emailing ThePerfectStranger in the evening. I didn't know what would drive me crazy first, the free time or the pain, but it was pretty neck and neck. They finally released me on Friday, and Uncle Ken said that his insurance would pay all medical bills and cover my wages while

I was in recovery, which would last months, according to my doctor.

I begged Uncle Ken to let me go work at the shop again—to do paperwork or something—but he said the wheelchair would get in the way. So, for the first time since grade school, it was just school and home for me.

Wolf made it his personal duty that first week to wheel me from class to class, even though I easily could have pushed myself. And he only ran me into other students a couple of times.

But on Friday, Wolf came up to Nora and me in American Government and said he wouldn't be able to give me a ride home because his band had a last-minute gig.

"You can't drive me home first?" I asked. "Mom won't be off work 'til eight. And Linda's busy with her own kids."

"I'll give you a ride home," Nora said.

I almost didn't believe she was talking, because her eyes were still on the position statement I'd written.

Wolf and I gawked at her, and she looked back at us, annoyed. "What?"

Wolf raised his eyebrows. "Nothing. Thanks."

He slouched off before I could argue. A ride home with Nora? That was like ice taking a ride with a ring of fire. Something bad was bound to happen to one or both.

"You don't have to," I said.

Her lips tugged back, like she was tired of me distracting her. "Are you planning on wheeling yourself home?"

I paused.

"I didn't think so." She made yet another note with her colored pen and handed the page back to me. "This is a decent start."

"Really? Because it looks like you bled on it."

She rolled her eyes. "Blood isn't pink."

I snorted. "Are you sure? I bet yours could be."

Her lips pursed in this cute, frustrated way. "Whatever."

Wait. Did I just think of Nora Wilson as cute? Again? Without insulting her after? What the hell was going on with me?

I coughed. "I'll get this fixed up."

She nodded. "Good. And will you read over my audience analysis?"

What had happened to Nora Wilson, and who was this girl in front of me? Was she seriously asking my opinion on her paper? But I didn't want another withering stare—even if it was kind of hot—so I took her paper and read it over.

When the bell rang, she turned on me. "Look,"

she said. "I have to get my sister to ballet practice in like ten minutes, so I don't have time for you to wheel yourself. Is it okay if I push you?"

I looked up at her. She had to be, what? Five-three? And she definitely weighed less than a buck twenty. Compared to me, she was practically one of those little yellow guys Janie liked to watch on TV.

"Can I?" she asked impatiently.

I lifted my hands. "Sure." This should be fun.

And to be fair, she did pretty well. But her sister was already waiting by the car when we got there, tapping her foot.

She looked at me. "What's going on?"

Nora pushed me by the passenger door so her sister had to jump out of the way to keep from getting run over. "I'm giving Emerick a ride home after I drop you off for ballet."

Amie met my eyes, and I gave her an apologetic wince. This was painful for both of us.

She shrugged and got in the backseat.

After I got in, Nora lifted the wheelchair in the trunk and hopped in the driver's side. And, let me tell you, she drove exactly like I thought she would. One mile under the speed limit, three-second pauses at every stop sign, and never once trying to make a yellow light. I could practically feel Amie's impatience in the back seat.

Amie got out, and Nora turned to me. "What are you smirking about?"

"Uh, nothing." Okay, that sounded stupid.

"Seriously."

"No." I snorted, thinking over her pulled five feet behind the stop line. "You're just a very...cautious driver."

She rolled her eyes. "You want another injury?"

I gestured at my leg. "This didn't happen driving, you know."

She raised her eyebrows. "Wolf said a car fell on you?"

I told her the painful story, and her eyebrows went up even further.

"See?" she said. "Texting while doing other activities can be very hazardous."

"I wasn't texting. I was checking my email."

She snorted, a delicate sound. "That makes a difference."

Indignant, I said. "It does. And stopping on the actual stop line isn't going to kill you."

"Maybe, but speeding might," she huffed.

"Oh really? Even three miles over the limit?"

She gripped the steering wheel and started backing out. "My driver's ed teacher said she got a speeding ticket once going one mile over the speed limit. And my parents told me one ticket and they'd take my license away."

Typical parent move. "Yeah, but then they'd have to drive your sister to practice."

Her mouth went slack, like it was the first time she'd ever considered the actual consequences of breaking the rules, but she didn't elaborate. "Okay, where's your house?"

I told her the cross streets, and she nodded. "Mind if we stop by my house first? I forgot my polo."

"What?"

"I volunteer at Mercy Hospital, so I have to wear a polo there."

I sat back in my seat. "That's fine." Not like I had anything to do anymore anyway.

We rode in silence for about fifteen minutes, and then she entered a gated neighborhood. The kind where each house was bigger than the last. My uncle's whole house could have fit into one of these five-car garages. Thinking about these rich pricks made me mad. Did they seriously need this much space?

But then we pulled up to one of those big houses, and I realized the girl driving me home was one of those rich pricks. Except she wasn't, entirely. Just the daughter of one. And she'd taken time out of her day to give me a ride.

"I'll be right back," she said and jogged into the house.

I tried to imagine the life she led inside. Her parents who cared about her, her dad who made the news for doing good things, her siblings who got to do fun stuff like dance and karate. And I tried to stifle all the jealousy I felt. Did they even appreciate all they had?

Nora jogged back out and got in the car, wearing her plain blue polo with the hospital's name embroidered right above her chest. "Okay."

She got going down the road, and we sat in silence with me occasionally giving her directions.

"So," she said, "are you excited for the field trip Monday?"

I shrugged. "It definitely won't be my worst day at school."

We pulled up to Uncle Ken's house, and I tried to see it through Nora's eyes. What would she think of the plain grass yard, the seven windchimes Aunt Linda hung on the front porch? Of the old, rusted station wagon sitting out front?

People like Nora and her dad acted like they served "the people," but how could they when they didn't know how people really lived?

"I'll get your wheelchair," Nora said and stepped out.

When she came to my side, I hopped down on one leg and settled myself in the wheelchair.

"Do you need help getting inside?" she asked.

I shook my head. "You're good to go."

She turned to leave.

"Oh," I said, "and thanks."

She gave me a small smile, got in her car, and drove away.

And for some reason I didn't totally understand, I was sad to see her go.

FOURTEEN

NORA

MR. ROBERTS CAME onto the bus with a wheelchair, and Emerick hopped up the stairs behind him.

"Nora's sitting over there," Mr. Roberts said.

I scooted over so Emerick would have room, and he sat down beside me, adjusting his cast under the seat in front of us.

Thank God it was just a short ride to the capitol. Emerick was already a tall guy, but this cast definitely complicated things.

After Emerick sat down, Mr. Roberts walked down the aisle and handed out paper packets to each pair. "This is the scavenger hunt I've prepared for you at the capitol. You and your partner will work to find the clues, and whichever team makes it to the final clue first with correct answers for the previous items wins. The first-place team will be able to represent our school at a student Q&A with our current governor, as well as a free season pass to Frontier City and White Water Bay this summer."

Students' faces lit up around me. Mr. Roberts should have led with the free amusement park tickets. It seemed like hardly anyone my age cared about politics, even though this stuff would be affecting them for years to come.

In the seat behind me, Trey spoke loudly with his partner, saying they had it in the bag.

I gritted my teeth and whispered to Emerick, "We are so winning this."

"Yeah?" He tugged off his leather jacket and set it on his lap, sending the smell of leather and cologne over me.

It made me think of Trey and the eighty-dollar cologne he wore that basically smelled like rich kid. Emerick smelled...real. Earthy. Down to earthy. Okay, I didn't know a good way to describe his smell, but we had a half-hour ride shoulder to shoulder. Surely, I'd figure it out.

Emerick looked me over, and I felt naked, even in my sweater and khakis.

"So," he said, "what's our strategy, boss?"

I kept my head forward to avoid those eyes that understood too much. "The main thing we need to do is think clearly. Everyone's going to be running around like chickens with their heads cut off."

He arched a heavy brow. "You ever seen a chicken with its head cut off?"

"It's an expression."

"So, no?"

I rolled my eyes. "No. Thank God. You?"

He shrugged and looked down at the packet. "Maybe we should think through some of the clues."

"Now you're talking."

We huddled over the page, and I furrowed my eyebrows. "What does 'head for the glasses' mean?"

Emerick frowned. "Maybe like a trophy case?"

"Hmm. It couldn't be actual glasses, could it?"

He shrugged. "Does head mean anything?"

My eyes flew open, and I put a finger to my lips.

An easy grin transformed Emerick's features. I never understood how a smile could make someone look so completely different, but I did now. It was like night and day on the same person.

We spent the rest of the trip quietly talking about the things we'd have to find and some of the major things at the capitol. Once we got there, Mr. Roberts gave us the long speech about us being seniors and needing to act like it, then let us loose. Emerick and I were already at a disadvantage, since he was in a wheelchair, but Wolf helped push him, so that was fine.

As we got closer to the building, I couldn't help but be in awe. I'd been there before with Dad, and even then, it seemed every bit as amazing as a cathedral with its enormous pillars and marble facade.

We went around the handicap-accessible entrance and through the metal detectors. Wolf's earrings set off the alarm, so Emerick and I ditched him while he got scanned with the metal wand. He needed to join his partner, anyway.

At the elevator, I pushed the button at least five times. Emerick and I were going to win this. But more importantly, Trey was going to lose.

We got to the second floor, and I pushed Emerick past the people taking selfies around the Native American statue. We went directly to the Hall of Governors, where bronze busts of all Oklahoma's governors lined the wall.

I couldn't see Emerick's eyes, but I heard the realization in his voice. "Which one has glasses?"

"I'll look left, you look right," I said.

"There!" Emerick pointed to one in the far corner.

We approached the one bespectacled governor, and Adam read the plaque. "Charles Bradford Henry.

Governor of Oklahoma, January 13, 2003 to January 10, 2011."

"Selfie?" I asked.

He nodded, and I lifted up the phone to snap a quick picture. Then I pushed him out of there, casually, acting like we were searching the walls nearby. We didn't need our classmates piggybacking on our ideas.

Emerick scanned the packet in his lap and read the next clue. "This is my sad room."

"Hmm." I tried to think over the rooms in the capitol and if I remembered any of them being named after Charles. But he'd been governor so recently, I doubted it.

Emerick scrubbed his chin. "Okay, let's think of blue, Charles, and governors."

I nodded, racking my brain for all the information I had stored of the capitol. Why wasn't this coming easier?

"Is there a private room for the governor?" he asked.

"None that would let an entire class in for a field trip."

"Okay, what about a room named after him?"

I looked toward the ceiling. Emerick was good at this kind of thing—really good. But I wasn't going to tell him that. "The governor's office is on this floor. Let's walk that way."

He rested his hands on his lap. "Let's go."

I rolled my eyes. "Okay, your Highness."

A deep chuckle lifted his shoulders. "Chop chop. Unless you want your ex to win."

Okay, that got me going. I pushed him to the governor's office, weaving around tour groups and people who worked there. The capitol was always busy when Congress was in session.

There wasn't anything at the governor's office, but we turned down a hallway.

"What's down here?" Emerick asked.

"The treasury." I kept pushing him but stopped as the idea hit my mind. "The Blue Room."

"What?"

As fast as I could without massacring us on the marble floor, I ran him to the big wooden doors at the end of the hall. We skidded to a stop, and I backed him in through the doors. We entered the gallery. There were pictures from the latest construction project going on downtown. A big company had decided to headquarter in OKC.

But I wheeled him to the adjoining room, with walls painted blue, floor to ceiling. I rested my hands on the handles and took it in—all the leather chairs, the fireplace, the beautiful western paintings.

"Who named this?" Emerick asked. "They run out of rich white dudes to celebrate?"

I snorted. "Good point." But then I remembered that my dad was just another "rich white dude" to Emerick and that I was just another rich white dude's daughter.

I took the packet to try and cover my frown.

"What's the next clue?" Emerick asked, blissfully oblivious to my sinking gut.

Steadying my breath, I read, "'This is old news.' Well, that's easy. The press room."

Emerick shifted in his seat. "There's a newsroom here?"

I nodded, forgetting he hadn't been here before. "Yeah, there are a few newspapers that have reporters working here."

He nodded, and that was the end of that.

After we took a quick picture, I pushed him toward the press room, and we took another selfie in front of the sign.

Our next clue said we needed to go house hunting.

"Easy," Emerick scoffed. "We just need to go see the House of Representatives, right?"

He really was good at this. I nodded. "But we can't go right to the chamber. We probably have to go to the public entrance."

Back onto the elevator. Another trip down a marble hallway. And then we were overlooking a room filled with men and women mingling. I recognized some of them from Dad's campaign functions.

Emerick and I snapped a quick selfie, then rushed out to find the next clue. *Do they really keep it 100?*

"Lame," Emerick said. "That has to be the Senate, right?"

"Yeah. Surely."

"What's Shirley got to do with it?" he asked, and I cracked up laughing.

"*Airplane?* Nice."

After going to the Senate's side, we mulled over the next clue. *What do fencers say?*

"What do you think?" I asked Emerick.

"I mean, in the movies, they always say, 'En garde!' Do you think we need to go back by the security guards?"

My jaw dropped. "No. You know what's on top of the capitol, right?"

"Um, an Indian?"

"Native American," I corrected, "and it's a statue called 'The Guardian.' That has to be it."

Emerick chuckled. "Have fun getting up there."

I snorted. "Did you miss the replica right where we came in?"

"You're wasting time yakking!" he said. "Where's the go button on this thing?"

Fighting a smile, I pushed him to the statue, and we took a selfie in front of it.

An older woman wearing a visor and a fanny pack grinned at us. "You two are such a cute couple."

Emerick and I looked at each other.

"Would you like me to take a picture?" she offered.

Before I could correct her and tell her Emerick and I were the last two people who could be dating, she reached for my phone. Not one to argue with a grandma, I handed it over.

I knelt down, and Emerick put his arm around my shoulders. The contact sent fire down my skin, and I tried to smile, even though my stomach was bouncing up and down on my small intestine. And the way he smelled...

"Here you go," the woman said, and Emerick moved his arm.

The spell was lifted just as quickly as it had started, and I was left dazed, trying to make sense of what had just happened. But we didn't have time for that. One clue left.

I read from the paper. "'You figured this out. You are the best.'"

I looked around and saw Trey and his partner taking a selfie in front of the statue.

"Hurry!" I said to Emerick. "Think. What is it?"

His eyes landed on the supreme court. The best.

I glanced over at Trey, and he followed my eyes.

"Let's go!" I yelled and started pushing Emerick.

I might have had a guy in a wheelchair for a partner, but Trey had a girl in a dress and high-heeled boots. Emerick and I were so winning.

I dropped my phone in Emerick's lap. "Get the camera ready!"

He swiped the screen up. "Ready!"

In the most epic maneuver I'd probably ever make, I spun Emerick around and grinned for a selfie. "Take it!"

Emerick's thumb pressed down on the button, rapid firing a bunch of pictures. We'd gotten it. Before Trey and his partner.

I slowed him to an uneasy stop and dropped to the floor, panting, happier than ever that I'd worn my Sperry's.

Emerick reached his fist out, and I tapped it with my own, grinning.

Trey walked over with his partner. "What's your time stamp say?"

Emerick handed me my phone, and I checked the first of nearly fifty pictures. "Eleven twelve."

He glanced down at his picture, and a curse word slipped through his teeth. "Eleven thirteen."

Trey cussing? He'd always made negative comments about kids who went around school using bad words. And now he was looking at Emerick and me with an openly disdainful stare. His jaw moved like he was about to say something, but then his lips curled up into the least smiling smile I'd ever seen.

He extended his hand. "Good job."

Emerick reached his hand out, but Trey ignored it. "I was talking to Nora."

FIFTEEN

EMERICK

I COULDN'T SEE Nora's face, but I felt my chair move under me and watched Trey's jaw drop as Nora wheeled me away from him.

She started muttering. "Dirty...rotten...scum bag..."

And despite myself, I laughed. "That's the best you can do?"

She stopped and came to stand in front of me with her arms folded. "What?"

I looked up at her. "Come on. There has to be a good cuss word or a bad name in there somewhere."

She tucked a strand of blond hair behind her ear, showing a pearl earring. "I don't cuss."

"Like ever?" I gave her a yeah-right look. I could think of at least five expletives for that asshat off the top of my head, and another fifteen if she gave me some time.

She shook her head. "Of course not. I have younger siblings, so I have to be a good example. And I'm the student body president. Cussing doesn't exactly go with the position."

Yeah, I'd expected the whole class president thing, but siblings? I thought of her two younger sisters coming to the hospital with her and found myself smiling like an idiot. So Nora didn't just do things to make herself look good. And the whole feisty, not-cussing thing was cute as hell.

But I'd do well to remember who she was here. A well-respected politician's daughter. And me... I didn't want to think about it.

She went back to stand behind my wheelchair. "Let's go find Mr. Roberts."

We went to the elevator and down to the first floor to find Mr. Roberts in front of the gift shop. After checking each of our selfies and congratulating us, he said we should go to the fifth floor and check out the Senator's visitor gallery.

Which we did. And it only took about fifteen minutes. And the ridiculousness of the whole situation hit me. Here I was, in this our state's capitol, with the daughter of Oklahoma's future governor, and we were looking at stuff on the visitor's packet?

"Come on," I said, "there has to be something better to do here. A secret passageway or something."

She lifted her eyebrows. "This isn't Hogwarts."

But I knew weird shit went down in politics. "There has to be something."

Her eyebrows came together over her dainty nose. "Well. I can show you the guts."

"Now we're getting somewhere."

She went back to the handles of my wheelchair and wheeled me to a service elevator. We rode to the basement, and she turned down a deserted hallway.

She started whispering, probably so her voice wouldn't echo off all the marble down here. "My sister Amie and I came down here during one of Dad's press conferences. Mom had her hands full, and we kind of snuck off." Even now, she looked a little guilty. "But they just told me to watch Amie, so I wanted to do something different."

"What do you mean?" I twisted to look at her, but she kept her eyes straight forward.

I thought she wouldn't reply, but finally, she said, "Off the record? It's not easy being Mom and Dad's built-in babysitter. I never get to think of me first or what might be fun to do, just what I need to do."

Who would have thought I'd be in the capitol building relating to Little Miss Perfect? "I get what you mean."

A small breath blew out her nose. "You have younger siblings?"

"No," I said, "but I have a mom."

"What do you mean?" I could practically feel her frown on the back of my neck.

"My dad...well, he isn't around."

"Like he left?" She sounded saddened by the thought.

And she was the first person who acted like I deserved any sympathy. Like I shouldn't just move on with my life and forget about the fact that my dad was probably being violated every day, that my mom cried herself to sleep on her brother's couch every night, that we both had to work ridiculous hours to pay off the credit cards Dad took out in her name because his credit was shit.

So I told her. "He's in jail. For at least ten years. Which means my mom will need me for at least that long."

The wheelchair slowed, and I felt Nora's hand on my shoulder. It seemed so small compared to my frame, but it had a huge effect, sending warmth from her fingertips all the way down to my toes. How could a simple touch through my leather jacket affect me more than Lacey-call-me-yours had with her entire busty chest pressed against me?

But Nora started talking again, taking me out of

my thoughts. "I get what you mean. I mean, I don't; my dad's still around, but he's gone all the time. We hardly ever see him. Sometimes I feel like my mom's a single mom to all five of us. There's not enough of her to go around."

Something Nora said, about her mom, about her sacrifice—it sounded familiar. And it felt like a lightning bolt ripping through me.

Could Nora be ThePerfectStranger?

I shook the thought. She couldn't be. ThePerfectStranger wouldn't have looked at me the way Nora did that day Mr. Roberts said we were partners.

She came to a stop in front of a metal door painted the same color as the walls. "This is it." Like a real-life Nancy Drew, she stepped forward and cracked the door open, pressing her eye to the gap.

Her entire body stiffened, hyper alert.

"What's going on?" I whispered.

She jerked her head back and shut the door. Without speaking, she went to the back of my wheelchair and started walking us briskly away.

My heart hammered, sending adrenaline through my veins. "Was there a cop?"

She let out a quiet bark of laughter. "No."

"What was it?"

She kept walking, the walls moving past us much faster than before.

"What was it?" I repeated, my nerves stringing tight. If we were going to get in trouble, I had a right to know what was going down.

But she ignored me, pushing away.

I put my hands on the wheels and held on tight, almost sending myself toppling over.

She shrieked, trying to keep me upright. "What the hell was that?"

I waited for her to come look at me before folding my arms over my chest. "So you can cuss."

Nora didn't just look mad; she looked livid. "You want to know what's going on?" she hissed. "I just saw my dad making out with a woman who was *not* my mom."

My jaw went slack, just as useless as my mind, which wasn't coming up with anything to say right now.

"Happy now?" she asked. "Or would you like to hear more? Maybe how he had her skirt hiked up and—"

"No, no, no," I said. "I'm sorry."

She looked over her shoulder, tears building in her eyes. But then she nodded, and her face got all perfect again. Like nothing was wrong. If there wouldn't have been a pool of liquid along her bottom lash, I might have believed her act.

Without another word, she went back behind me

and started pushing. It was the most awkward ride to a gift shop I'd ever had before, and that included the time Dad took seven-year-old me along to be the distraction while he robbed the one at the Oklahoma City Zoo.

Nora didn't talk to me the rest of the field trip, not when Mr. Roberts congratulated us in front of the entire class, not when we got back to the school, not when I told her I'd text her about our next assignment. But then when we got off the bus, she whispered to me, "Don't you dare tell anyone."

And then she left me to call on Wolf to help me get back into the building.

As Wolf wheeled me over the rough parking lot, all I could think was, fine. *Fine.*

If Nora wanted to go back to ignoring me, she could. It didn't affect me. Not really. We could do our homework assignments separately, go back to pretending each other didn't exist. Fine.

But somehow, I knew it wasn't. Because there was a chance Nora was ThePerfectStranger, and everything I'd felt for Stranger would be everything I'd felt about Nora. The real Nora—the depths of herself she didn't show anyone else. And I knew, deep down, like I knew my dad would eventually end up in jail, I knew Nora wouldn't want a thing to do with me once she found out who I was.

I waited all evening for an email from ThePerfect-Stranger, and right at nine, it came.

From: ThePerfectStranger
To: ADAM
Adam, are you up? I need your advice.

From: ADAM
To: ThePerfectStranger
Want to use Google chat?

A message popped up in the bottom corner of my screen.

ThePerfectStranger: Hey
    ADAM: Hey Stranger
    ADAM: What's up?
    ThePerfectStranger: Oh, you know, the sky is falling down and all that.
    ADAM: Hard day, Chicken Little?

ThePerfectStranger: I almost forgot that movie! I need to show it to my younger sisters.

ADAM: You're getting off topic.

ThePerfectStranger: Sorry. It's weird to be messaging you, you know?

ADAM: Yeah. It is. It makes you seem more real.

ThePerfectStranger: Exactly.

ADAM: So... Wanna talk about it?

ThePerfectStranger: I mean, yeah. That's kind of why I messaged you.

I didn't know what to say to that, so I waited, and eventually her bubble popped up again like she was typing.

ThePerfectStranger: So, I saw something today that could destroy my family and really hurt my dad's career.

My fingers shook as I typed out the next message.

ADAM: What did you see?

And then I prayed for literally the first time in my life, begging some omnipotent, invisible superhero to swoop down and change the words that were about to flash across my screen. *Please don't say you saw your dad cheating. Please don't say it.*

ThePerfectStranger: I saw my dad kissing someone who was not my mom.

I pushed my computer back off my lap and sat on the edge of my bed with my head in my hands.

Nora was ThePerfectStranger.

How hadn't I seen it before? The goodie-goodie who does everything right, complaining about family stuff. Begging for advice anonymously because she wouldn't dare hurt her perfect image. Of course it was Nora.

But part of me wanted to hold on just a little longer to this person I'd built up in my mind.

ADAM: Does anyone else know about it?

ThePerfectStranger: You mean other than my dad and that bimbo?

ADAM: Yeah, other than them.

ThePerfectStranger: My partner on this class project knows.

I pinched the bridge of my nose. This couldn't be happening. Out of the thousand people we had in our high school, Nora Wilson was ThePerfectStranger? And she had no idea who I was...

ADAM: Could you talk to your partner about it? Get his take?

ThePerfectStranger: He's not exactly the guy you go to for advice on family stuff.

My chest tightened, and I scratched at the spot right over my sternum.

ADAM: What do you mean?

ThePerfectStranger: He's just...not like you.

ADAM: ???

ThePerfectStranger: I guess, if I wanted advice on how to hot-wire a car, he's the guy I'd go to, you know? If I told him about my daddy issues, he'd just laugh in my face.

God, I'd been the biggest idiot, pining away over this "stranger." She only saw me as a good-for-nothing bad boy, just like everyone else. Even though I'd lain in the hospital with a shattered leg working on that stupid project, she still thought of me as no better than the gum under her shoe. But I'd have to reply, or she'd know it was me, and I wasn't risking my diploma over Nora Wilson.

ADAM: I think this is above my pay grade. Maybe talk to Mrs. Arthur about it.

She might have replied. She might not have. I wouldn't know, because I slammed my computer screen closed and laid down.

I threw my arm over my eyes, but all I could see were Nora's words etched into my mind.

SIXTEEN
NORA

THEPERFECTSTRANGER: I don't need to talk to Mrs. Arthur. I need to see a friend. I know you were on the fence, but can we please meet up? Just for a little bit?

My heart squeezed, desperation threatening to take all the air from my lungs. Why had he thrown up a wall? I needed him now more than ever.

But I couldn't keep walking around the block forever, waiting for Adam to reply. Partially because my parents would start getting worried and partially because my heart hurt more with each second that passed without his reply. His silence communicated even more clearly what words could have said: I'm not interested.

This entire day had been awful. Yeah, Emerick and I had beat Trey at the scavenger hunt, but I'd lost so much more. And I had a feeling this was just the beginning.

I got closer to our house, and the driveway came into view, along with the Jeep parked beside my Crossover. Trey's brand-new Jeep with big tires and pearlescent white paint. Sure, I used to feel cool sitting in the passenger seat, but now I saw it for what it was: just another meaningless status symbol.

All the pain in my heart turned to anger. I was going to tell Trey once and for all to get out of my house—out of my life.

I expected to find him in the kitchen, but I only saw Mom there. "Where's Trey?"

She dunked her tea bag in and out of her mug. "I said he could wait for you in your room." Her face looked pinched.

"Mom, are you okay?"

She folded her hands on the table. "Yeah, my stomach's just upset."

I wanted to ask why her eyes looked so tight or why her lips turned down at the corners, but I had other things to tend to. "Okay. Goodnight."

She nodded. "Goodnight, sweetie. Don't let Trey stay too late—you've got an early morning."

Just like always. But I agreed and went upstairs.

The door to my room was closed. Ugh. I hated the idea of all my stuff being subjected to his presence. I twisted the handle and pushed my door open.

Trey sat on the edge of my bed, his hands in his lap, but he seemed frazzled. I checked around my room. My laptop was closed on my desk, none of my books seemed to have been moved, my dresser drawers were firmly shut. What had he been messing with?

"Trey, what are you doing here?" I asked.

He stood up and came to me, but I took a step back.

He frowned. "Nora, I wanted to give you another chance to take me back. I know there's been some...animosity between us, but I'm ready to put it behind us if you are."

I rolled my eyes, and it felt good. I could see why kids did it all the time. "Trey, I don't need another chance. I need you to get out of my room."

He took another step closer and put his hands on either of my arms. "Nora, don't do something you'll regret later."

"Is that a threat?"

"Are you seeing someone else?" His stare was so intense, it felt like I was under interrogation lights.

"Even if there was someone else, it wouldn't be any of your business, because we're broken up."

"Nora, I—"

"No." I shook out of his hands and held the door open. "Get out of my room," I hissed. "Get out of my house. Get out of my life. And leave me the *hell* alone."

Trey's face hardened to blazing stone, and he practically spat his next words at me. "You just made a huge mistake, Nora Wilson. Just wait."

He jogged down the steps and left the house without even telling Mom goodbye.

I sagged onto my bed, exhausted. Trey's threat had felt real, but I was too tired to worry about it.

A soft knock sounded on the doorframe, and I looked up.

Amie stood in her sleep shirt and barely-there shorts Dad hated. Her blue eyes were wide. "Are you okay?"

The back of my throat stung, and I swallowed. But I couldn't talk, so I just shook my head.

She came to my bed, sat down beside me, and wrapped her arms around my shoulders. She didn't talk, just held me like that and let me cry.

If I could have found the words, I would have told her how lonely I felt—how the one guy I actually cared about didn't want to meet me. That our parents' marriage was crumbling right under our mother's oblivious nose.

I just wanted to be a good big sister, a good

friend, but I felt like I was failing at that, too, because my little sister was comforting me when she should have been sleeping.

Instead, I let her comfort me. She helped me under my covers, and I fell into a deeper, darker sleep than ever before.

For the next few days, I refreshed my phone as often as I could, checked my email on my laptop, and updated my Gmail app, hoping to hear from Adam. But no messages came.

This wasn't machine failure or a glitch with the app. This was a flaw in me. Why else would Adam talk to me for so long but not want to see me? He knew me better than anyone else. He knew me enough to stay away.

London and Grace asked what was wrong, but I couldn't tell them the whole truth. Just that I was taking the breakup hard. Which was mostly a lie, but it was also kind of true. I wished I could go back to six months ago, when I thought Trey was perfect. When I hadn't seen his ugly side. When I thought my dad was a good man.

Now, my whole world crumbled underneath me, and I didn't know how long I could keep hopping over emotional landmines before getting swallowed whole in the parting ground below me.

But I never knew how bad it could get.

On Thursday morning, London stormed up to me in homeroom, Grace in tow behind her. London's heels pounded on the tile, and she brandished a school paper. "What the hell is this, Nora?"

My eyebrows furrowed. "*The Ledger?*"

She opened it so hard it was a wonder the pages didn't rip in half. And then she started reading in a whiney voice. "*My friends just don't get it. They have their lives together. I couldn't tell them about my ex or my parents or family stuff. We just talk about hair and make-up and boys. Not real things like I do with you.*"

I snatched the paper from her and looked at the headline on the front. *MAKING UP FOR OUR MISTAKE, A special issue dedicated to Nora Wilson.*

On the front page was an editorial written by Trey. I scanned it, barely making sense of his words over the pounding in my head.

Part of being a good journalist is maintaining a high level of integrity and honesty in reporting. That means owning up to mistakes when they are made. When Nora Wilson and I suggested the advice column, Dear Adam, we meant for it to be representative of the student body and for all students who needed help to receive it. In addition, we wanted students to see the issues of other students. Essentially, by sharing these struggles, our student body would feel less alone. Unfortunately, those who lead often let their own self-care slip between the cracks. Nora, I would like to publicly apologize for not ensuring you received the help you needed from our columnist. No letters to the advice column should be hidden, no matter how "perfect" things may seem on the surface. Please, accept this apology from the entire WAHS Ledger staff, and seek out the help you need.

Your WAHS Ledger editor,
Trey Walters

Not wanting to believe it, I flipped through every page, including the twelve-page insert with all of my emails spelled out in Times New Roman. The one small grace? Trey hadn't included my latest instant message thread with Adam.

Where had Trey found the emails? Had Adam been behind this?

I couldn't worry about that now. I had to find Amie before she could read the emails and see what I'd said about her, our family.

The loudspeaker clicked on. "Will Nora Wilson and Trey Walters please go to Mrs. Arthur's office? Nora Wilson and Trey Walters, please go to Mrs. Arthur's office, immediately."

It clicked off, and I stared at London and Grace, their hurt expressions. "Let me explain. Later."

London inclined her head toward the paper in my hands. "I think you said it all."

Our homeroom teacher walked in, a copy of the paper rolled up in his hand. "Nora, did you hear that?"

I nodded and brushed by my former friends to go to Mrs. Arthur's office.

Trey reached her door at the same time I did, and there wasn't a glare strong enough in the world to do this moment justice. I hated Trey with every fiber of my being. He was a dirt bag, not worthy to take up space with the gum underneath all the desks, not worth all the rotting food in a dump.

And the worst part? He was grinning at me, satisfied with everything he'd done.

There weren't regular words strong enough to describe exactly how horrible of a person he was. "Eat shit," I said, just in time for Mrs. Arthur's door to open.

She and Principal Scott stood in the room, Mrs. Arthur holding on to the door handle.

Principal Scott folded his arms across his chest. "Come in, Miss Wilson, Mr. Walters."

Mrs. Arthur shut the door. "Sit down, please, both of you."

I dragged my chair as far away as I could get from him, which wasn't far in this tiny office, and knocked a bobblehead over.

I picked up the tiny, grinning Bob Stoops, and put it back on her desk. The thing nodded happily, and I just wished he would stop grinning at me like that.

Mrs. Arthur went to sit behind her desk, but Principal Scott remained standing, his arms folded across his bulky chest. "Care to explain yourself, Mr. Walters?"

Trey sat up in his chair, looking like the perfect example of a "good kid." If anyone had been looking in, they'd probably think he was getting an award, dressed in his khakis, a plaid button-up shirt, and leather Sperry's. Even his hair was gelled and styled to perfection.

"Sir," Trey began, "like I mentioned in my editorial, this school has done Miss Wilson and her peers a severe disservice. As you can see from all the letters she sent, she has been in great distress and suffering silently."

Principal Scott grunted. "Cut the crap, Walters."

Trey's head jerked back like he'd been slapped. Adults never talked to him like that. "Excuse me, sir?"

Principal Scott put his hands on Mrs. Arthur's desk and leaned forward until he practically towered over Trey. "You abused your power as editor and humiliated Miss Wilson over a breakup."

Trey's eyes flitted everywhere but at Principal Scott.

"Are you aware of how much your little stunt cost the school? We won't be able to run the paper for three weeks now, thanks to you."

Trey finally looked up. "I can pay it back."

"You mean your parents can?" I muttered.

Principal Scott lifted a finger. "Hold on a minute, Miss Wilson." He turned back to Trey. "Your parents are on their way here while we come up with a punishment fitting for your behavior. You get back to class and think about what you did. And you better come up with a good excuse, because something like this is grounds for expulsion."

Trey could get expelled?

His mouth dropped open. "Expulsion? I'm the student body vice president, captain of the basketball team, and editor of the newspaper," Trey said, outraged. "You want to explain to the entire school why you threw away a state championship?"

Mr. Scott's lips went thin, and he leaned so close to Trey, I bet Trey could feel the principal's breath on his face. "Are you threatening me?"

Trey's eyes shifted down. "No, sir."

Principal Scott stood up. "Good. Get out of here."

Trey walked outside, and the door closed behind him. Suddenly, the room felt small, and I felt dizzy with all the bobbleheads nodding around me.

Now, Mrs. Arthur spoke. "Nora, I'm so sorry about this."

I folded my arms tightly and stared down. "Can I go talk to Amie?"

Mrs. Arthur nodded. "Mr. Scott, will you page her?"

He left the office, rubbing my shoulder on the way out. Like I could have felt any more pathetic.

The sound of a paper rustling made me look up. Mrs. Arthur had the day's issue in front of her. "I know these were your private emails, but there's a lot of hopelessness in here. Have you ever heard of Caregiver's Fatigue?"

"If you read all the emails, you would know the answer," I said, bitter. I'd warned Adam against it in my very first email.

She pursed her lips. "Well, we're on the same page. It's perfectly normal for someone in your position to let self-care slide. When your mother gets here, I'm going to recommend she give you a day this weekend just to take for yourself. I know it won't fix everything, but it might be a start."

"Wait," I said. "What? My mom's coming?" My stomach sank. Mom would know about the messages. What I said about her being a single parent and giving up her dreams. "You didn't tell her about the emails, did you?"

Mrs. Arthur's big head nodded up and down like all of these stupid bobbleheads. "You can't suffer through this alone."

"I'm fine," I lied. "Look, I've got to talk to Amie before she sees everything."

A knock sounded on the door, and Principal Scott walked in, alone.

He cleared his throat. "Amie...refused to meet with us."

Mrs. Arthur looked so sad for me, and I hated it. Something in me snapped, shifted, broke, became something I couldn't recognize. And all I could see was this blurry doll smiling at me, nodding like everything was fine.

I picked up the Bob Stoops bobblehead right in front of me and ripped his stupid smiling face off. And then I ran out of the office, to the parking lot, and got into my car where I could cry without grinning faces nodding at me like everything wasn't completely ruined.

SEVENTEEN

EMERICK

"WHY'S EVERYONE READING THE PAPER?" **Wolf** muttered to me in homeroom.

I shrugged. "Exposé on the dangers of unprotected sex?"

He snickered. "What? That's dangerous?"

I rolled my eyes. "Yeah, dude."

"Gotta take care of that baby gravy, yo." Wolf stuck his hand out for a fist tap, and I hated myself for returning it.

I laughed. "You're so weird."

Someone called for Nora Wilson and Trey Walters over the intercom, and I looked at Wolf, confused.

He shrugged. "Probably won some award for getting their heads farther up their own asses than anyone else in history."

"Yeah," I said, laughing, but my heart wasn't in it.

Nora might not be who I'd imagined ThePerfect-Stranger to be, but some part of her was real. Unfortunately, the realest part of her thought I was a brainless delinquent on his way to juvie.

We sat through the whole "mindfulness" crap, which was basically just a good excuse to sit around and not think about anything for a while. Honestly, it was kind of nice to have some time at school where you didn't have to hear kids talk shit on each other or get useless info drilled into your brain.

Rolling into the hallway after homeroom was like watching one of those weird old horror movies where everything was normal but terribly wrong. Everyone had their noses in the newspaper.

Wolf snagged one out of a freshman's hands and held it up.

My mouth fell open. Right there in black and white were all of the emails Nora Wilson had ever sent me. And all of the emails I had sent her, for the entire high school to see.

And Trey Walters talking about integrity? That was the most ridiculous thing I'd ever seen. Mrs. Arthur had to know he was the one who did this, not me. It wasn't just Nora's reputation at risk now. It was my entire future.

"I gotta go, man," I said to Wolf and wheeled through the crowd of distracted students. I had to find Mrs. Arthur before Trey could get the story twisted.

When I reached the door to her office, I heard yelling inside.

"You're talking about expelling my son? He is a model student, a star athlete, and has been a dedicated servant of this school!" a man's voice roared. "So the kid got his heart broken. What do you expect? How was it even possible for him to make such a big change to the order of the paper? Aren't there any checks and balances at this school?"

I wheeled closer to the door, listening to every word. This guy had to be Trey's dad, and by the way he was acting, no wonder Trey was such a rage-suppressed dick.

Principal Scott started talking, not yelling like Trey's dad. "The *WAHS Ledger* is a student-led publication. Our teachers edit the final version of each week's paper and that file is sent to the printer. Your son—"

"My son," the man said, his voice still loud, "my son will be graduating from this school in May. You can find a punishment that seems fit, but it will not be expulsion. If you make the wrong choice, I can guarantee a legal battle like this school's never seen before."

"Is that a threat?"

"No, it's a promise."

The door banged open, and I saw who I assumed to be Trey's dad first. He looked just like Trey, but with gray hair and a rounder waistline.

I casually leaned back in my chair, like I was supposed to be there, not in class like every other student.

On Trey's way out, he caught my eye and sent me a glare so hard, you'd have thought he'd learned it from my dad.

"Emerick," Principal Scott said.

I jerked my gaze from Trey's back to see Principal Scott standing in the doorway.

"Come in," he said.

He held the door open as I wheeled in to Mrs. Arthur's intense gaze. Suddenly, I felt like I was in a fishbowl. I couldn't stand the bobbleheads.

The OU one was right in front of me. The only one that wasn't nodding.

"What happened to Stoops?" I asked.

Mrs. Arthur picked him up and rolled the separate pieces over in her hands. "Nora got to him."

Now I liked her even more. Great.

Principal Scott dropped into the chair beside me, looking completely exhausted. He rubbed his eyes, then blinked them quickly. "What a mess."

"You're telling me," I muttered.

Mrs. Arthur sighed. "Emerick, I—"

"Wait," I said. I needed to get my part out first. "Look, I didn't want to do this advice column at first, but I started to like it. I'm good at it. I have thank-you emails from students. And Stra—I mean, Nora, she was a good friend to me. I was never going to tell her who I was or reveal anything about the other students." And then, I did something I'd never done before. I asked for mercy. "Please, don't expel me. I need to graduate."

A small smile touched Mrs. Arthur's lips. "I know. You're going to graduate."

Shocked, I looked between her and Principal Scott, who nodded.

"But we're cancelling the advice column," she said.

And for reasons I didn't understand, that sounded worse than not graduating at all. "What?"

She twisted the broken bobblehead so its mug swiveled all the way around. Just when I thought those things couldn't get any creepier. "Considering today's events, we don't think students will trust writing in, at least this year, and after we recoup the costs from Trey's stunt, we'll only have a few issues left anyway."

"What about an online issue?" I asked.

Mrs. Arthur's eyes bored through me, calculating.

"That's an idea we'll consider. But I'm afraid our Dear Adam experiment is done. You're off the hook, and as long as your identity as Adam remains a secret, you'll graduate in May."

I looked to Principal Scott. Was Mr. Hard Ass really going along with all of this?

He nodded. "Don't you have a class to get to, Mr. Turner?"

All of the bobbleheads around me already knew the answer, but I said it out loud. "Yeah."

But there was no way I was going.

I sent Wolf a text message, and he met me by a side exit. Ditching was always easier when I had two functioning legs, but we still managed to get to the parking lot without notice.

Movement from a few cars over caught my eye. Nora sat in her SUV, her head leaning against the steering wheel, shoulders shaking.

I twisted my head to look at Wolf pushing me from behind. "Hey, man. Wait in the car. I gotta take care of something."

Wolf's eyes shifted back toward the school. "What?"

I tilted my head toward Nora's car. "Just wait."

He stopped the wheelchair, and I pressed my hands against the cold cars in the parking lot to help me hop over to her vehicle. God, I couldn't wait to advance to crutches. Finally, I hopped to lean against the passenger door of Nora's SUV, and I tapped on the window.

She jerked up, but turned her head away first, wiping at her cheeks. Then she faced me, looking surprised.

Had she been expecting someone else?

She pushed a button, and the window slowly came down. "What's up?" she asked, casual, but the pain in her eyes had my chest aching with her. No one deserved to have all their shit splashed on the front page. Not even Little Miss Perfect. And especially not ThePerfectStranger.

"You okay?" I asked.

Stupid question.

She gave a quick nod that totally wasn't convincing. "I'm fine," she added. "What are you doing out here?"

Her message from the other night about me hotwiring a car flashed through my mind, and I wished I had any answer for her other than skipping school. But maybe this could be a good thing?

"Wolf and I are getting out of here," I said. "You wanna come?"

Her eyes looked somewhere beyond me, and I followed her gaze. A minivan had parked in one of the visitor spots up front, and this total MILF got out. She immediately went to the back doors and reached in, probably getting kids out.

"That's my mom." Nora jerked her chin up. "In a few minutes, she's going to go into the school and sit down with Principal Scott. And she's going to learn about the newspaper and all of the horrible things I said about her behind her back when I was acting like the perfect daughter to her face."

"Nora, it'll—"

She held up her hand, her blue eyes looking dead. "You don't get it. You don't know what it's like for people to actually expect something from you."

That delicate grip she had on my heart? Yeah, she squeezed, twisted, ripped that thing right out of my chest. This fantasy I held on to in the back of my mind? It belonged in the garbage with the rest of me. Because that's all she saw me as—trash.

I nodded and turned away, wanting to sprint out of there. But my leg wasn't good enough for that. Just like the rest of me.

The second I got into Wolf's El Camino, he peeled out of the parking lot, and I'd never been so glad to get away from the school. May couldn't come soon enough.

He drove, didn't even bother telling me where, but eventually we parked at Dolese Park. In the summer, trees would give us cover, but right now, all the leafless branches were still trying to decide whether it was time to bud or not.

He got out of the car, came around to my side, and let me put my arm around his shoulder. Together, we hopped to the little lake and sat on a bench.

You know the worst thing about writing an anonymous advice column that left your entire future hanging in the balance? Having your hard-core best friend take you to a spill-your-guts place and not being able to tell him what's going on.

He opened his jacket and lifted a flask from his pocket. "Need a drink?"

I snorted and looked around. "You tryin' to get in trouble?"

Wolf shrugged. "What's it matter?"

"Maybe I'd like to spend my day somewhere other than the police station." We spent enough time there last year for dumb shit—ditching school, hitting parties, smashing mailboxes on Halloween. He should know better by now.

"What's going on with you, man?" he asked. "You've been weird as hell since school started back."

"What do you mean?"

He lifted his eyebrows. "I mean, you never ditch anymore—other than today—you don't even look at girls anymore, you're all quiet and always looking at your phone... What is it?"

I shrugged my jacket up and pulled it tighter. "Nothing, man."

"You gay?"

I shoved him. "No. You don't have to be gay not to date." And then I pulled a Nora line. "You don't get it. You're still a junior. You've got another year of this. After May, I'm done. I have to decide if I want to do something with my life. Messing around with you and the guys is fun—it can't last forever."

Wolf scowled. "You think I don't get it? My parents remind me every freaking day that this music thing is shit. They tell me the odds are against me and I'll end up some broke old dude."

"Yeah, but the drugs and stuff? You think that's rock and roll or some shit?"

He sneered. "Shut up."

"No." I shoved his shoulder. "Get your act together, Wolf. You want this music stuff? Go for it. Don't blow your chances messing around with stupid shit."

Wolf turned toward the lake and stared over it for a minute, his jaw working. "I'm tired of being a fuck-up."

"Then don't be."

After a moment, he snapped up from the bench and reached into his pockets. The silver flask flew through the air and landed in the lake. A couple small ziplocks followed. And then Wolf jumped in, clothes and all.

We didn't talk much after that. Just drove around, bummed some free food from the place where he worked. And then he dropped me off at home. But something was different. Not just in me, but in him.

I went to my room/the garage/the laundry room and pulled out my laptop. I should email Nora, as the guy she actually liked, tell her I was sorry. But when I tried logging into the Dear Adam gmail account, it said the password was incorrect. And when I tried to recover it, it said the access email was Mrs. Arthur's. Or, that's who I guessed me*********ur@wahs.org was.

I still remembered Nora's fake email, but that would mean emailing her as myself or making another fake Adam account, and my heart just wasn't in it. She'd made her point, loud and clear.

So, I opened my regular email, and my eyes landed on one message between ads for clothes and restaurants.

The Oklahoman had emailed me back about the internship.

From: The Oklahoman HR
To: Emerick Turner

Dear Mr. Turner,

Thank you so much for your interest in the position. Unfortunately, we have decided to move forward in our search with other applicants.

Best of luck,
The Oklahoman Team

EIGHTEEN

NORA

THE ONLY THING worse than having your innermost thoughts put on display for the entire high school? Seeing them talked about on the four o'clock news.

Dad clicked off the TV in the living room, and I put my head in my hands. This was bad. Bad. Bad.

"Look at me," Dad snapped.

Mom rubbed my leg. "Honey, Nora's—"

"No," he said, waving his hand holding the remote with a sense of finality that couldn't be argued. "Nora, how could you be so stupid? What have I always told you?"

Each of his words stung to my core. He was right. How had I trusted a complete stranger with all of my secrets? And where was Adam now? He certainly hadn't come forward to apologize. No, he'd left me to deal with Trey's attack, all by myself.

"Well?" Dad said.

Like reciting the alphabet, I said, "'There's a reason they call it a private life and not a public life.'"

"Right," he said. "This campaign can only work if the entire"—he waved his hands in wide circle —"family is on board. Each of us has a part in this, and all of us have made sacrifices." He paced across the carpet in front of Mom and me, gesturing angrily as he walked. "Your mother works herself from dawn until dusk taking care of you girls. Amie is excelling in ballet, making a positive name for herself in the arts community. Opal never questions what to wear to events. And we counted on you most of all. You let us down. If you ruined my chance at becoming governor, I'll never forgive you."

He wanted to talk about forgiveness? Sacrifice? Maybe he could explain what role his basement rendezvous with that woman who was not his wife had to do with his run for governor. Or with supporting this family.

I turned my eyes up at him, burning with humiliation and rage. "If Hillary can forgive Bill, you can forgive me."

Did he hear the threat in my voice? I couldn't tell.

He narrowed his eyes. "You are in big trouble. I won't be able to campaign for the next week and a half because I have to stick around here during your spring break!"

Angry tears stung my eyes. "What a shame, having to spend time with your own family."

Dad's phone went off and he held it to his ear, listening for a moment. "Yes, I heard it...It's a complete disaster...We'll be there in thirty minutes."

He hit the end button and stared at me. He kept his voice low. "You will go upstairs and change into a respectable outfit, you will put on make-up, and you will get down here in fifteen minutes so we can go to FOX25 and try to do some damage control."

I stared at him, and he snapped his fingers. "Now."

I gave one last look at Mom, who'd just sat there the whole time and let him rampage, and ran toward the stairs.

Opal stood a few steps up, and when I met her eyes, I saw nothing but sympathy and worry.

I bent over and kissed her forehead. "Love you, girl. Don't worry about me."

But I ran upstairs before she could say anything back.

In front of my mirror, I took deep, cleansing breaths like we'd learned in homeroom, but it seemed futile. The truth was, I meant all of the things I'd said to Adam. I had wanted my dad to be around more, to make pancakes on Sunday morning like he used to, to play catch with us in the park, to not constantly worry about what we said or how we dressed. But now, I didn't know that man downstairs. I couldn't reconcile the dad I missed to the slime I'd seen cheating on his wife in the capitol building. Couldn't believe his DNA made half of me.

But I picked myself up, because I was a Wilson, and that was what we did. We put on a happy face and acted like things were okay when they were anything but.

Mom and Dad met me downstairs, and they left Amie in charge while we drove to the news station. We went through hair and make-up and sat down with a reporter on a set made to look cozy and inviting with cushy chairs and a painting in the background. The shining overhead lights and microphone hooked to my lapel told a different story.

Dad's PR guy stood with us on the set. After talking with Dad, he came to me. "Okay, here's what you need to say, kiddo." He handed me a sheet of paper, and I read over the bulleted list of talking points.

My dad is my hero.

Senior year is tough. Everyone needs someone to talk to.

My parents taught me family means more than anything.

My sisters are my best friends. I would do anything for them.

I'm excited to go to OU so I can stay close to my family.

Vote Wilson for Governor.

As I read down the bulleted list, my gut clenched.

"Want to practice them?" he asked.

I shook my head. "I'm fine."

"Good."

The reporter came on stage and shook hands with each of us. And when the camera man counted down, I transformed into the daughter I knew Dad wanted. The one who effortlessly served her family, school, and community. The one who really thought her dad deserved to be governor.

But as soon as the lights turned off, that girl was gone. The only thing I knew was that I loved my sisters. That I had to make things right with my friends. And that, even though I'd been broadcasted to thousands of people, the person I really wanted to talk to was Adam.

Spring break was a nightmare. Dad made each of us kids volunteer with him at the soup kitchen every single day. It would have been fine if we were actually there for a good reason, but Dad just wanted to save face.

Amie still hadn't forgiven me, hadn't talked to me. Actually, she made Opal tell me anything she had to say. Real mature, I know. I had Opal tell her so.

The worst part? Mom was so sweet and comforting to me when Dad wasn't around. She left little encouraging notes in our lunches, came and said goodnight every evening, and told me I didn't have anything to be ashamed of. Trey did. She said every teen needed someone to vent to and that Amie would come around.

But while she said all these things the perfect mom would say, I held her and Dad's marriage in the balance. Should I tell her? Was it my place? I didn't know, and it was tearing me up inside, especially when I didn't have Adam to lean on.

Friday night, I lay in my room, staring at the ceiling, when Dad walked in.

"I'm heading out," he said.

I rolled my head to the side to see him leaning against the doorframe. "See ya."

"Want to try that again?"

"Goodbye?"

He nodded and scuffed his toe on the carpet. "Look, Bug, I know you think I'm tough on you, but it's just because I think you've got something special.

Some of nation's greatest leaders were oldest children whose parents pushed them to be the best they could."

Any other time, I would have eaten that up, dreamed about my future with him, but now? When I knew who my dad really was?

"Everyone slips," he said, "it's owning up to your mistakes that matters, and I think you did that this week."

The corner of my lips twitched into a half-hearted smile. I just wondered when he would do the same.

He turned to leave, his hand still on the frame. "See you Tuesday."

"Drive safely."

I closed my eyes and listened to him say his quiet goodbyes to the other girls. When I heard the front door close behind him, tears leaked out my eyes because now I didn't know where he was really going.

I tried to go to sleep, but no amount of sheep or deep breathing or counting backwards from two hundred was enough to still the storms inside my mind. This night called for something more.

I slipped out of bed and padded quietly down the stairs in search of the only thing that had helped me sleep when I was waiting for the results of my own election for student body president—a peanut butter and banana sandwich with chocolate milk.

Halfway through mixing in the Hershey's syrup, I heard someone else walk into the kitchen.

I turned to see Mom, wearing her silk pajamas.

"Couldn't sleep either?" she asked.

I shook my head. "Want some chocolate milk?"

She nodded, and I made her a glass too.

We sat together at the breakfast bar, sipping our milk. Oceans of lies and secrets hung between us. Could she feel them too?

"One day left before school starts," Mom said.

"Don't remind me." Sunday, we'd have church, and then it would be back to the routine of packing lunches, taxiing the kids around town, and facing people who knew everything about me.

She rubbed my shoulder. "It'll be okay, honey. If anything, I think it could be a good thing."

I stared at her, open mouthed. After the big deal Dad had made about the leaked emails, how could any of this be considered a good thing?

"You know, sometimes the worst thing isn't the worst thing," she said. "Remember when you had the idea for the advice column? You said you wanted people to feel like they weren't alone, and I bet having other kids see that you struggle too, even though your life might look pretty good from the outside, could be really good."

I'd never thought of it like that. "But I'd trade it

all just to go back to how things were." Oh, how I wished I could do that.

She smiled softly. "We can't go back. We can only go forward, knowing what we know, and make the best of the situation."

I chewed on my sandwich, thinking about that. Knowing what we know.

Knowing what I knew, I needed to tell Mom. She didn't deserve to live a life built on a lie.

I set my sandwich down and rubbed my hands on my pajama pants. "Mom, can I tell you something?"

She brushed my hair behind my ear. "Anything, honey."

A lump grew in my throat, and no matter how hard I tried, I couldn't swallow it down. I had to talk over it. "When I was at the capitol, I saw Dad with another woman."

Her eyes went blank. "What do you mean?"

"I was in the basement, showing my partner around, and I saw Dad kissing someone else."

She tilted her head to the side. "Are you sure it was him?"

I nodded, and she sighed.

Sure, I didn't have much experience in this department, but was that how she was supposed to react? Why wasn't she crying? Throwing his things on the front lawn? Calling him to confront him?

"Mom?"

She looked back at me like she was just remembering I was in the room. "Honey..." She pressed her lips together, thinking. "Marriage is...complicated."

And then it dawned on me. "You knew he was cheating on you?"

Her hand went to the back of her neck, under her ponytail, and she looked down for a moment. "Yeah, I knew."

"What?" If I'd thought my world was crumbling before, it was vaporized now, built on a foundation of sand.

She put her hand on my knee, but it felt all wrong. "No marriage is perfect. When you get married, there will be things about your spouse that you don't like, and you'll have to decide what compromises you're willing to make. Your father is an excellent dad to you girls, always pushing you to be better. He provides for us, works hard to make sure we have a good home, that Amie can do ballet and you can volunteer without needing to get paid, that Opal can do karate. And just because he's straying now, doesn't mean he always will."

Every word she said sounded more wrong than the last. How could she say what she did with such conviction? How could we go to church as a family every Sunday when Dad was breaking the number one premise of a Christian marriage?

My chin quivered, and I stood with the remains of my sandwich, my milk, my faith. "I'm going to bed."

Her eyes were soft. "Okay. Just know no matter what, your dad and I love you girls more than anything else. That will never change."

I nodded, sending tears down my cheeks. I dropped my food in the trash, my milk in the sink, and I went upstairs before she could see how thoroughly her words had sliced through me.

Instead of turning right at the top of the stairs, I turned left and went into Amie's room. I'd lost the people I thought my parents were. I couldn't lose my siblings too.

She stirred the second I walked inside, and she sat up, looking at me in the soft light coming in through her window.

"Amie, I'm sorry," I sobbed. "I love you more than anything. Just forgive me. Please, forgive me."

Silently, she lifted her blanket and let me crawl in bed with her. I slid under the covers and wrapped her in my arms.

"I love you," I said. "And I'd never trade you or the others for anything."

She buried her head in my shoulder. "Promise?"

I nodded, against her cheek. "Promise."

NINETEEN
EMERICK

LIVING IN A GARAGE/LAUNDRY room really sucked. Especially when I just wanted to be alone. Every time Aunt Linda did a load of laundry—which was a lot since she had three kids and a husband who owned a mechanic shop—she checked on me. And not just, "Hey, how are you doing?" No, she made sure to ask if I needed food, if I wanted some water, if I wanted her to push me around the block for some fresh air. The kind of stuff my mom might do if she wasn't working 24/7.

Don't get me wrong; it was nice as hell. Just not when you wanted to lie around and do nothing for a week.

The door opened, and I prepared myself for another run-in with Linda, which basically meant pretending to sleep, but this time, a little voice said, "Emerick?"

I opened one eye to see Janie standing in the doorway. "Yeah?"

She came into the garage and closed the door behind her. "It's the last day of spring break." She said it like that was supposed to mean something to me.

"One more day of freedom," I said.

She smiled. "You mean boredom."

Janie was weird like that. The kid loved school.

"Yeah," I said, "that's what I meant." I scooted over on my futon, and she lay down with me, staring at the ceiling.

"Why do you hang out in here so much?" she asked.

I shrugged. "Nothing better to do."

"Don't you lie to me." She sounded surprisingly like her mom. "I know Mama's been inviting you out to the park and stuff."

How was a ten-year-old already so good at shaming me? "You know, you'd be a great cop."

She smiled. "Or a forensic investigator."

I scrunched my eyebrows. "How do you even know what that is?"

"Read about it in a book."

"Ah," I said.

"Really. What's going on?" She rolled her head to the side and looked at me. "You sad? I read a book about depression, and—"

"Where are you getting these books?"

She looked a little sheepish. "Borrowed one from Mama's shelf."

I smiled, and I wanted to tell her I wasn't down, that everything was fine, but I couldn't. So I settled for the truth. "I applied for a job, but I didn't get it."

A frown transformed her face. "What job?"

"Promise you won't laugh?"

She crossed her heart.

"I applied for an internship at a paper."

Her eyes lit up. "Like a writer?"

I nodded. "Exactly like that. But I didn't get it, so I guess whenever this leg heals up, it's back to the shop."

All the light in her face morphed to confusion. "Why would you go back to the shop if you want to be a writer?"

"'Cause I need a job."

"Then just apply at another paper." She said it like it was so obvious.

"It's not that simple, Janie," I said.

Her little eyebrows scrunched together. "Sure it is. Just keep applying." She put a hand on my chest.

"If you want it, you'll make it happen." She smiled at me. "Make us proud, Rick."

I pulled her in for a hug. "You're too smart for your own good, kid."

"Thanks. Oh, and Mom says supper's ready." She held my hand and led me to the dining room, obviously under strict orders to get me out of there. I didn't know who was smarter—Janie or Aunt Linda, but I was nowhere in the running.

That evening as I lay on my futon, Janie's words and childlike faith stuck in my mind. *If you want it, you'll make it happen.* Who was to say she wasn't right?

A knock sounded on the door. Ma. She walked in and sat on the end of my bed. I sat up too.

"So," she said, smoothing out the end of my blanket. "Janie tells me you want to be a writer."

I waited for it—the judgment, telling me that writing wasn't a real man's job, that I'd be poor forever.

"You know," she said. "I think that would be a fine career. You should go for it."

"But what about you?"

She shrugged. "What about me?"

Then I asked the question I had to ask. "What if I get a job someplace else?"

Smiling, she patted the bed next to her. Slowly,

awkwardly, I sat next to her with my massive cast hanging off the side.

She took my hand and looked at me, her eyes heavy and tired but intense. "You know, I'm the mom, and you're the son. And I think we'd both be better off if we remembered that." Taking in a deep breath, she stood up and looked down at me, a soft smile on her lips. "Goodnight."

"Night, Ma."

After she left, I looked around the garage. Why was I taking on so much responsibility for Mom? She'd never asked me to. Uncle Ken would give her a place to live as long as she needed it. I could send her money from wherever I went, and I wouldn't need much to survive on. As I pulled up the job boards online and searched for newspaper jobs—any newspaper jobs—I started to think, for the first time in my life, that this could actually happen.

For the next few hours, I filled out application after application, starting in Oklahoma and eventually moving my search out of state. But even after my eyes grew tired and my fingers felt numb, there was still one thing I missed. ThePerfectStranger. But there wasn't anything I could do about that.

Or was there? Something Stranger—Nora—had said about being yourself no matter what others thought stuck out in my mind. Nora might have thought I was just a run-of-the-mill bad boy, but I wasn't. I was Adam. I just needed to show her that.

Even though it was eleven, I sent her a text asking if she wanted to meet up to plan out some of our assignments. Maybe if I kept showing her how dedicated I was with school, it would make a difference.

Within a minute, she replied.

Nora: Let's meet tomorrow morning? 7 at the school?

And even though it meant begging Aunt Linda for a ride, I said yes.

When I walked into the library the next morning, Nora was already at a desk, thumbing through her book. She didn't see me walk in, so I just stood there for a little bit, watching her...like a creep, but what the hell.

Her blond hair fell over her face, and she pushed it back, leaving a patch of her neck, her porcelain skin exposed. Did it feel as silky as it looked?

She bit her full lips together and furrowed her eyebrows, then made a note on her paper.

Yeah, I'd known Nora was hot before, but how had I not realized the cute way she stared at books like the words were the only thing in the world? Or how the ends of her hair fell just below her shoulder blades, tickling the middle of her back? I wondered what the strands would feel like slipping through my fingers. What her hair would smell like.

God, I was a creep.

I walked closer to her and lifted my hand. "Hey."

She looked up, then at her wristwatch. "You're five minutes early?"

Eight if she counted the three I stood around watching her, but that was beside the point. "Yeah." I went and sat next to her at the desk. She had nearly a page full of handwritten notes. "What were you working on?"

"I wanted to start an outline for our opening speech at the debate," she said. "And I wanted to tell you something."

That little line formed between her eyebrows again, and it took all of my effort not to reach out and smooth it down. "What is it?"

She tipped her chin down, then looked at me under her lashes. "I wanted to say I'm sorry for how I acted last Friday, when you came to check on me. That was...really nice of you, and I just wasn't in a good place."

Was she being honest? Her big, blue eyes just begged me to believe her. "It's fine," I said. "Everyone says stuff they don't mean."

A storm cloud crossed her eyes, bringing moisture

with it. Panic rose in my chest. Had I said something wrong?

She lifted her hand and wiped at her eyes. "Ugh, I'm sorry." She sniffed. "It's been a long week."

I rubbed her shoulder, not sure if that was the right thing, but she didn't shy from my touch. "I bet it's been rough."

She laughed, bringing on a fresh round of tears. "You have no idea. You know what we saw on the scavenger hunt?"

We were deep in unchartered territory, so I just nodded.

"My mom knows about it." She stared at me, unanswered questions in her eyes. "She knows about it, and she's not going to leave."

Not planning it, not thinking about it, I pulled Nora into a side-armed hug. "That sucks. I'm sorry."

A sob shook her shoulders. "I used to be able to talk to Adam—whoever he is—about things like this, but now my friends are mad, and I can't tell my sister, and I don't have anyone."

She cried for a little bit, and even though it felt like her pain was leaking through my jacket, straight into my chest, it felt good to be there for her since I couldn't as Adam anymore.

We didn't get much work done that day, but

something better happened. Nora went from being my social studies partner to being my friend.

For the rest of the week, we worked together to smooth out our speech, and on Friday in class, we went to the computer lab with our classmates to design campaign posters. And, trust me, this was all Nora. I couldn't draw for shit, and I was about fifty percent sure I was colorblind. Or at least color deficit. If that was a thing.

Wolf came up behind us and looked over my shoulder at the poster Nora had made. "Dude, that's awesome."

Nora grinned. "You think?"

"Totally," he said. "Hey, you think you could make one for me?"

We both turned to look at him, shocked.

"Not for this class." His cheeks looked a little red. "I'm gonna start giving kids guitar lessons."

I reached back and clapped his shoulder. "Corrupting youth. Nice move."

He shrugged my hand off, laughing. "Nah, Imma be good."

And I believed him. Since his random swim in the lake at Dolese Park, Wolf had been different. Yeah, he still cussed and picked up gigs at bars, but I never wondered if he was high or not. And he actually stayed with me after school to work on homework when he didn't have a shift to work.

Since we still had about twenty minutes in class, Nora started on a design, and I had no idea how, but she made this bomb poster for him and sent twenty copies to the color printer.

She lifted an eyebrow. "Perks of being student body president."

Yeah, regular Nora was hot, but taking-advantage-of-executive-privileges-to-help-my-friend Nora was irresistible.

Wolf looked like a kid on Christmas morning with the stack of warm flyers. "Hey, can you find another ride after school so I can go post these around?"

And since Nora was right there, and since she was nice, she volunteered.

After the final bell rang, we met by the front doors and went out to her car. She drove me to Uncle Ken's, apparently remembering how to get there from last time.

What could I say? The girl was smart.

She pulled along the curb and looked over at me. "Here you are."

I smiled at her, probably looking dopey as hell. "Home sweet home."

Her lips twitched, almost forming a smile. "Hey, I

just wanted to say, I'm sorry for being such a snob when we were first partnered up. You've actually kind of been the best project partner I've had all year."

And I didn't know whether it was the compliment or the smell of her hair—strawberries and mint if you were wondering—but I had everything I needed to do the craziest thing I'd done in all my life.

"Will you go to prom with me?"

EMERICK. Turner. Just. Asked. Me. To. Prom.

Breathe.

But that was a bad idea because I just got a massive heady whiff of his leather jacket and earthy cologne.

All the obvious alarm bells were going off—the ones that said Emerick and I lived parallel lives, never destined to cross, but here we were, sitting in my car, a question hanging in the air between us.

And I was blowing it because I couldn't just open my mouth and give him an answer.

If I was being honest, it wasn't all the pent-up teen angst and bad-boy persona that was holding me back, because something in Emerick had changed since that day I collided with him. He was...different. A great lab partner, kind, and not as rude to me about being a rich kid as I was to him about being a delin-quent. Even though I'd totally misjudged him.

No, the thing—person—holding me back was Adam. I missed him. Missed the idea of him. Adam had never been as real as this guy sitting across from me, all dark eyes, lean muscles, and this vulnerable brokenness that showed through no matter what tough exterior he put forth. How hadn't I noticed it before?

Emerick looked down at his hands resting in his lap, and I realized there weren't grease stains there anymore. He couldn't work with his leg.

He sighed. "You don't have to say yes. It was—"

"No," I said. "I mean, yes. I want to go with you."

One of those transformative smiles covered his face, making a light dance in his dark eyes. "Yeah?"

I smiled right back. "Yes. I'll text you later with details?"

His eyebrows scrunched like he didn't quite understand. Guys never did.

"You know, dress color and stuff like that?"

"Oh," he said. And if his skin would have been as light as mine, he might have been blushing. But that was just a guess. "Awesome."

If I smiled any more, my face would crack in half. "Awesome." I hopped out of the car and took in a deep breath of the fresh spring air. It smelled like everything amazing. Possibilities, new life, maybe something more.

I went to the trunk and got his wheelchair, and he met me in the driveway.

"When does your cast come off?" I asked.

He cringed. "I have a surgery the Monday after prom. Another eight weeks in a cast after that, and then I'm good to go. If everything goes well."

That sounded awful, but Emerick had been through enough. He deserved better. "I'm sure it will."

He nodded and settled into the chair. He looked over his shoulder and met my eyes. I wondered what he saw when he looked at me. If all the letters in the paper had changed his mind about me.

"I'll see you later?" he said.

I nodded. "See you later."

As I drove away from Emerick's place, I couldn't get the smile off my face, and I knew I wanted to tell someone. Well, two someones.

For the first time in my life, I called in sick to my internship and drove back to the school. I sent out one text message to a group chat that hadn't seen anything in more than a month, even before the leaked emails had ruined everything.

I had to do better.

Nora: London, Grace, I'm in the parking lot. Please come talk to me.

And then I waited, but even though the texts had been marked as seen, neither of them replied.

Nora: Please. I'll wait out here as long as it takes.

They made me wait. I scrolled through social media, flipped through my assigned reading, texted Emerick the color of my dress and asked where he'd want to eat before prom, said a prayer the girls who'd been my best friends since third grade would find it in their hearts to come and talk to me.

A knock sounded on the passenger window, and I jumped. There was London in her workout clothes, and Grace stood right beside her.

I hurried to press the unlock button. London got in on the passenger side, and Grace sat in the back seat.

Cue the most awkward silence ever.

Sure, I'd thought about what to say, but none of it sounded right with both of them looking at me, not just mad, but hurt.

"I'm sorry," I tried.

London folded her arms over her chest and looked out the window, but Grace looked right at me. "Why couldn't you just talk to us?"

I looked down. "I just didn't want to be Nora Wilson for a while. With Adam, it was like I could be honest without worrying about what it would do to my reputation." My throat burned, and I swallowed.

London sighed, still looking out the window. "You don't always have to be the rock, you know. Sometimes it's okay to let people see that you're actually struggling with something."

Her words echoed my mom's so much it tore me apart. "Well, you want to know what's going on? My dad's cheating on my mom, and she knows it. I'm going to OU because I have to, not because I want to stay in Oklahoma. And, yeah, I love my sisters, but sometimes I just want to be their big sister, not their second mom." Fresh tears stung my eyes, and London turned to look at me, but I had to keep going. "And I miss my friends. I was the biggest idiot ever not to talk to you guys about what was going on. I think I just wanted someone to still see me as perfect, even when everything was falling apart."

London's big eyes filled with concern. "No one's perfect, babe. Especially in high school."

"Are you kidding me?" I asked. "You're an amazing cheerleader, going to a division one college in the fall. Grace is going to *China* to teach English to actual orphans this summer, and here I am, falling apart."

London put her hand on my knee, and Grace put her hand on my shoulder, holding me together.

Grace rubbed her hand in a circle. "We're here for you, no matter what."

London nodded. "And trust me, no one's perfect. You know my little brother just came out of the closet? My mom cried for a month."

"Yeah," Grace said. "And I'm going to prom with Fabio. As friends. Again. I think he felt sorry for me."

I laughed through my tears. "You guys have gone to every prom together."

Grace rolled her eyes. "That's one for the year-book. Grace went to every single prom with her best guy friend. Never had a boyfriend."

I smiled at her. "Maybe you'll meet some humanitarian hottie this summer."

She shrugged and looked between London and me. "No more secrets, okay?"

We both smiled and said "okay" at the same time.

For a moment, we sat there in a three-way hug that made me feel like things were finally back in place.

"But if we're not keeping any more secrets," I said and paused. "I'm going to prom with Emerick Turner."

Their eyes went wide, and London broke out into a grin. "He's going to be way more fun than Trey was."

I smiled. "I'm counting on it."

"Did you hear about Trey?" Grace asked.

I shook my head. "I haven't seen him in school since...well, you know."

Grace nodded. "So he got suspended from the basketball team, he's not the editor or vice president anymore, and the only reason he was able to come back to school is because his parents donated back all the money he cost the paper. They're starting the paper up again next week, but cancelling the advice column."

"How haven't I heard any of this?" I asked.

London shrugged. "I just found out after school today."

My stomach twisted. The paper was back. Without Adam. I took in a deep breath. There was one more thing I needed to do.

London, Grace, and I sat and talked about prom and life and things we'd missed until I had to go pick up Amie. And for the first time in a long time, it felt like everything was fine. Well, almost.

At home, I went up to my room and sat at my desk in front of my computer, and I wrote a letter to Adam. And just like the rest of our letters, this one had to go public.

TWENTY-ONE
EMERICK

THE LOUD SPEAKERS CLICKED ON. "Will Emerick Turner please go to Mrs. Arthur's office?"

I glanced over at Wolf. Seriously?

"What'd you do?" he asked.

I rolled my eyes and unlocked my chair. "Nothing."

His eyes glinted. "Yeah, sure."

I left our class and wheeled to Mrs. Arthur's office. The only thing I was happy about was that there would be one less functioning bobblehead in there, thanks to Nora. My prom date.

I still couldn't believe that. First, that I was going to prom at all. Second, that my date would be the student body president, perfect white girl Nora Wilson. Dads warned girls like her against guys like me.

I reached Mrs. Arthur's office and knocked on the door.

"Come in," she called.

Principal Scott waited inside with her. Honestly, I was starting to wonder why they didn't use his office more often. At least I wouldn't have to have all these dumb figurines nodding at me. But whatever.

"What's up?" I asked, stopping in front of her desk.

She held up this week's paper. "Have you read this?"

"Not yet." Honestly? I hardly read it even when I'd actually written for it. Now that I was getting about a rejection letter a day from newspapers, it was hard to read the things without having hard feelings.

She flipped it open and slid it across the desk to me. "I think you should read the letter to the editor."

I looked between her and Principal Scott. "You called me in here to read the paper?"

She smiled. "Just read it."

So I scanned the headline.

Student sings praises for Dear Adam

For the last two months, I've written many emails to our advice columnist, Adam, and for the same amount of time, he's written back. He didn't have to, I told him so right from the beginning, but he took his personal time to help me, a friend. For that, I am supremely grateful.

Not only was the issue of the paper sharing our personal emails humiliating, it was also cruel. Those private emails didn't just hurt me, they risked Adam's anonymity, and they hurt people I love deeply. But that's not what this letter is about.

Losing Dear Adam is a tragedy to this school. See, when I first found out about all of my private life being made public, I only thought of myself. But someone close to me reminded me that everyone struggles. Everyone in this school is going through something, whether you're a brand-new freshman or the student body president. We need Adam and his column so we'll never forget that.

Adam, thank you for everything you've done for me, as an advice columnist and as a friend. Thank you for being a great listener, a great confidant, and thank you for all the services you've done for this school.

Sincerely,
Nora Wilson aka ThePerfectStranger

My throat got tight, and I swallowed. I pretended to read for longer so I could compose my expression, but finally I dropped the paper on the desk.

Mrs. Arthur met my eyes. "Emerick, if you're willing, we'd like to have you back for the rest of the year."

This couldn't be real. For the last two weeks, I hadn't just missed Nora's emails. I'd missed the column. Yeah, at first the column was just about graduating school, but it'd become so much more than that.

I looked at Principal Scott. "Really?"

He cracked a rare smile. "I'll take that as a yes?"

I broke out in a grin. "That's a yes."

Mrs. Arthur slid a piece of paper toward me. "This is the new password." She glanced at Principal Scott. "And there's one other thing we talked about."

My stomach sank. Here was the catch.

"The anonymity clause," she said. "We've decided there might be an exception. With Nora. We think she deserves to know who she's been talking to, but it's completely up to you."

I glanced down at my hands. The column. Nora. It was a lot.

"Was that all?" I asked.

Mrs. Arthur nodded. "Yes. You can go back to class."

Before I went into English, I logged into the

Dear Adam email account on my phone. There were so many messages that would take time to go through, but my eyes landed on the most recent one.

From: Nora Wilson
To: ADAM
Dear Adam,

Please check the letter to the editor on Friday. I meant every single word.

I understand now why we couldn't meet, but I hope someday I'll be able to look you in the eye and tell you how thankful I am.

Nora

If only she knew how many times she'd looked me in the eyes.

I couldn't talk to anyone about whether to tell Nora

or not. Well, except Nora. And that would kind of defeat the purpose.

So, I wrestled with it, one moment wanting to tell her in class, the next thinking Adam should stay a secret forever. But finally, I decided. If prom went well, I would tell her. If not, well, I would leave our relationship in cyberspace, where it belonged.

But with the amount of shit girls needed for prom, there was about a seventy percent chance the night wouldn't go in my favor. Maybe. Between the flowers and the suit and the meal and transportation, I had to ask Aunt Linda for help, and I still wasn't sure I had it all. For ThePerfectStranger—Nora—it was worth all the trouble.

I sat in the living room with my entire family— Mom, Uncle Ken, Aunt Linda, Janie and the boys, and Wolf, who wasn't related but still wanted in on the freak show.

"Janie," Ma said, waving a disposable camera, "go take a picture with Rick."

Janie came to sit next to me on the couch, and I pulled her onto my lap so we'd be on the same level.

She pressed her cheek to mine and made the cheesiest grin. After a few flashes, I set her down.

"When can we meet your girl?" Janie asked.

"Yeah," Wolf said. "You gonna bring her over?"

I glanced around the living room. It wasn't bad, but

it wasn't the mansion Nora lived in with her family. If this was going to go anywhere, she'd have to see it all. Besides, it wasn't like I was ever going to be some rich guy. You know, print journalism and all. And I hoped she was the kind of girl who would see past all of that.

Hadn't she already by saying yes?

"You can meet her soon," I said.

Janie jumped up and down.

A horn sounded outside.

Ma looked at me. "That your ride?"

I scooted sideways on the couch and looked through the blinds. A big, black limo waited by the curb, looking more out of place in this neighborhood than I did in Nora's. "It's the group's, yeah," I said.

Nora's dad had rented it for the night. And it was about to take me to her house, to meet her family.

"One more picture with everyone," Ma said.

I smiled. "Sure." This was a first for all of us.

Wolf stood on the other couch, ignoring Aunt Linda's scowl, held out his phone, and took a selfie of our whole crazy crew.

Wolf stuck out his hand. "Go get your girl."

I slapped his hand and drug my fingers back. "You know it."

And then I hopped to the door, sat in my wheelchair, and rolled down the sidewalk. The driver helped me into the massive back seat and left me there, terrified to see Nora, and scared as hell to meet her dad.

On the drive across town, I stared out the tinted windows, watching the houses go from small to normal to massive. My heart pounded. This was the night. I realized I wanted to tell her about it all, to finally come out as Adam to the one person who'd seen me for me. But I had to do this first.

The limo came to a stop in her driveway, and I hopped out before the driver could open the door for me. That would just be weird. Besides, he already had to get my wheelchair out of the trunk.

And then I wheeled up the perfectly clean, not-cracked sidewalk to her front door. Before I could knock, a little girl had it pulled open. She looked a little bit older than Janie, and her smile instantly calmed my nerves. "Emerick?"

I nodded.

She swung the door open to the living room, and I saw Nora's little sister first. Amie.

She folded her arms across her chest and looked me up and down. "You look way better without the leather jacket."

I wheeled myself in farther and saw her dad's nervous look. "Leather jacket?"

I shrugged and stuck out my hand. That's what white kids did on dates, right?

It must have been good enough because Nora's dad stuck his hand out and shook mine. He had this presidential smile that didn't quite meet his eyes. "Nice to meet you, Emerick. Nora will be down in a second. You can come sit in the living room with us."

I pushed myself to a spot between two chairs and felt like I was sitting in a fishbowl. Four girls, including Nora's mom, stared at me, along with Nora's dad.

Nora's mom had a smile like Nora, though. Warm. "Would you like a cookie?" she asked, gesturing at a plateful on the coffee table.

Man, I was out of my league. "Sure," I said.

But I shouldn't have, because when Nora walked down the stairs looking like a freaking goddess, my mouth fell open, dropping crumbs into my lap.

Smooth move, Emerick.

I swallowed and brushed them off. "You look..."

"Beautiful," her dad finished.

Nora's mom went to hug her, and the two looked almost like they could be sisters, not mother and daughter.

After I slipped the corsage on her wrist, they took pictures of Nora, pictures of Nora with her sisters, pictures of Nora and her parents. With all the pictures not including me, I was starting to wonder if I was a fly in their white ointment family. But I shook that thought. Thinking that way never got me—or my dad—anywhere. Not anywhere good.

Nora gave me a pained look, then slid out from under her dad's arm. "Am I going to get any pictures with my actual date?"

Her mom laughed. "Sorry, Emerick, five girls means lots of photo ops."

I grinned. "I'm just happy to get in on one." But I didn't want to be sitting in a chair for this. I hopped to stand on one leg, and Nora let me put my arm around her waist. Her tiny waist that curved under smooth silk...

Dude, chill. Her parents are around.

I grinned for a picture or twenty, and finally, her mom reminded us that there was a limo waiting in the driveway.

"Ugh," Amie said, "I wish I could go."

Her dad looked at her. "No dating until you're sixteen. You know the rule."

Amie dropped onto the chair, looking pissed, but her dad ignored her. "Let me wheel you out, Emerick."

I tried to protest, but he wasn't having any of it. He pushed me out the door behind Nora, who looked even better walking away in those heels that clacked on the sidewalk. Her dress revealed almost her entire back, and the only thing that kept me from imagining touching the soft skin of her shoulders was her dad's breath hitting the back of my neck.

Awkward.

The driver let Nora into the car, and she gave me a final smile before getting in. In just a few seconds, it would be her and me alone in this massive back seat. It was every guy's dream come true, but for whatever reason, it was happening to me. Was I ready?

Her dad wheeled me to the trunk, and I started to get out of my chair, but he put a hand on my shoulder. Keeping his voice low, he said, "You treat her right, you hear me?"

The threat in his voice came across clear, even if he didn't actually say anything menacing. Everything in me wanted to rebel against her dad. Basically the definition of The Man stood over me, his hand on my shoulder. What the hell did he think I could do that was worse than what he was doing to his own wife?

But this was Nora, and he was her dad, and I nodded.

He came in front of me. "You know, I don't trust that you know what that means."

I lifted an eyebrow. I might be in a cast, but I had to outweigh him by at least forty pounds. Try me, old man.

He held up his hand and started counting off. "No sexual touching, no hotel rooms, no leaving the prom before it's over, no leaving with any other girl, you got me?"

"You forgot the most important one," I said and got up from my chair, so I could look him in the eyes.

"And what would that be?" he asked.

I nodded my head toward the back of the limo. "Don't break her heart."

He eyed me for a moment, but his features seemed to relax, even if slightly. "That's right, now get in the car." He folded up the wheelchair and put it in the trunk, and I went to the back door.

I opened it and looked in to a hell of a sight. Nora, leaning back on leather in her soft pink dress that brought out the color in her creamy skin. God, just seeing her had turned me into a romance novel narrator. But surprisingly, I didn't mind. Not one bit.

When I sat down next to her, she said, "Dad gave you the talk."

I chuckled. "Yeah."

She shook her head.

And now, I didn't know what to do with my hands. Should I put my arm around her? Were we into hand-holding territory? Lacey-call-me-yours hadn't made me guess like this. She'd been very clear what she'd wanted me to do to her. And what she wanted to do to me. Maybe that was what made it so easy to say no.

Nora wasn't Lacey. Nora, this beautiful girl with blue eyes that made her look so innocent and...nice...sat next to me, her legs crossed so I could see her shoes. Most girls wore these spikey things to prom, but hers had a heel on them that wouldn't impale me. A heel she could dance in.

Oh God. I hadn't thought this through. Nora was the kind of girl who danced at these things. I was sure of it. How in the hell was I supposed to slow dance with her in my wheelchair? And why hadn't Wolf mentioned this along with his other smart-ass remarks?

"We're picking up Grace and Fabio next," Nora said.

"Fabio?" Aunt Linda had enough worn-out books with a long-haired, bare-chested dude on the cover for me to know who he was.

Nora giggled, and the sound was cute as hell. "You know who he is?"

"Yeah, but I'm pretty sure he wouldn't slum it at a high school prom."

She laughed again, and I swore in that moment I'd never get tired of that laugh, never stop trying to hear it again.

TWENTY-TWO

NORA

"HE GOES TO SCHOOL HERE, and his grandma is a *really* big romance reader," I said. We only a had a few minutes left of just Emerick and me. Before this little bubble popped.

When he came to pick me up, I couldn't believe how good he looked. Sure, he had the leather-jacket wearing, bad-boy look down to a science. But this? Emerick in a suit and tie? Jaw, meet floor.

I scooted a little closer to him, just enough that I could smell his cologne and feel the warmth of his side against mine. "You look really nice," I said.

He put his arm around me, and my nerves went crazy. My body had never reacted this strongly, even when Trey was kissing me, and Emerick could do it with a simple touch through his jacket sleeve.

Emerick's grin made the tingles grow even

stronger. "You look amazing." His voice was low, husky...hot.

Someone get me out of the kitchen.

"Thanks," I said, looking up at him.

The pad of his thumb traced a circle on my bare shoulder, short circuiting my brain. All I could do was grin up at him like an idiot. Where had Smart Nora gone, and who had replaced her with this giggling idiot?

"You know," Emerick said, "I'm really glad you said yes."

"Me too." How could I have missed out on how kind his eyes were? How they gave away his soft side, even when the rest of him screamed danger?

It all felt too surreal. The only thing that would have been crazier than me going to prom with Emerick Turner was me going to prom with Adam, and that was just about as impossible as spring breaking on the moon.

The limo slowed to a crawl and stopped outside of Grace's house. Emerick gawked at it out the window and tried to hide his expression, but not soon enough.

"Her dad has this patent," I said. "He's just a banker now."

He blinked, clearing his features, and nodded.

What was going on in his mind? Sometimes he

could just wipe his expression without a moment's notice. Where had he learned that?

I followed his gaze out the window and saw Grace walking down the sidewalk, looking stunning in a blue sheath dress that clung to her tiny frame. Fabio walked beside her, tall and lanky, a goofy grin on his face as usual. Grace was the only one of us girls with a guy best friend, and sometimes I was jealous she had a built-in date. Not tonight though, with Emerick at my side.

When the limo door opened and Grace saw us, she broke out into a huge grin. She scooted next to me and took in my dress. "Oh my gosh, you look amazing." She glanced at my date. "And you look great, Emerick. You did an awesome job on the color."

He said thanks, giving her an uneasy smile.

Fabio sat about a foot away from Grace. "Looking good, you two."

"And you!" I said. "I love the cummerbund. Classic."

"Yeah." He frowned. "It was my grandma's idea." He shook his head, replacing his frown with a goofy grin. "Okay, I have the perfect thing to spice up this party."

I lifted my eyebrows. London, Grace, and I had made a pact freshman year not to drink until we were twenty-one, and as far as I knew, none of us had broken it, or intended to.

Grace eyed him. "What is it?"

A sly smile took over his features. "Let's wait for London."

No matter how much Grace and I prodded him, he wouldn't budge until London was in the car, countless layers of tulle spread out around her.

Emerick leaned into my shoulder, and his breath tickled my skin. "Where's her date?"

I turned to speak in his ear, and he was so close, I swore I felt electricity radiating from his skin. "Her boyfriend's in college."

Grace hit Fabio's knee. "Okay, what's the plan."

There was that mischievous smile again. "It's kind of like truth or dare mixed with bingo," Fabio said, "but it's only dares, and you have to do it during the dance." He scanned the rest of us, probably looking for any hints of rebellion.

London shrugged. "Fine, but Nora picks the dares."

Grace laughed. "Nora's the worst at dares."

My cheeks heated. "I am not the worst."

They both folded their arms across their chests. Honestly, it was kind of creepy.

Grace nudged Fabio. "I told you about the time

she dared me to eat M&Ms before bed so I'd get a cavity, right?"

He snorted.

Okay, now my cheeks were even redder, and I was very much aware of the sexy guy snickering next to me. "You told him that?"

London crossed her legs, and her dazzling stilettos caught the light. "That's nothing." She looked at Grace. "Remember the time she had me make that A look like a B and show my mom so I'd get in 'trouble'?"

I covered my face. God, they could have just taken some lipstick and written LOSER on my forehead. It would have had the same effect.

Emerick nudged my shoulder. "You did that?"

Still keeping my hands over my face, I nodded.

He pulled on one wrist and twisted his fingers through mine. "That's so cute."

And sure, I would have rather been sexy or beautiful or stunning, but cute coming from Emerick, in that low, smooth voice? I'd take that a million times over.

Fabio raised his hands. "Fine, fine. Nora's dare has to get approval from the group. All in favor say aye."

A chorus of "ayes" rang in the back of the limo, and I squeezed Emerick's hand. "Whose side are you on?" I whispered.

His lips curved into an easy grin. "I'm on the side of having an awesome night with you."

"Well, when you put it like that..." I smiled.

"Okay, okay," Fabio said. "I'll go first." He pulled a notebook and pen out of his pocket and started writing. "Kiss somebody."

All of a sudden, Emerick's lips seemed more prominent than ever before. Would those lips be touching mine before the night was over?

London gaped at him. "I have a boyfriend who isn't here."

He rolled his eyes. "You don't have to get all of them." He finished scribbling with a flourish. "Next."

Grace took the pad. "Get between a couple dancing too close and tell them to make room for Jesus."

Emerick's chest rumbled with laughter. "I'm totally doing that in my wheelchair."

London acted like she was raising the roof. "Yessss!"

Fabio clapped his hands. "You get it."

Grace handed Emerick the notepad, and he started writing. I read the words as he wrote them: "Grind on someone else's date."

For the millionth time, my cheeks felt warm. Grinding? That was basically dry-humping to music.

That town in Footloose was starting to look more appealing than ever.

Emerick handed me the notepad, brushing my fingers again. Like a static shock, electricity bounced between us. My eyes met his. Did he feel that too?

I took in a deep breath. Time for a good dare. "Tell someone how you really feel about them."

Fabio's mouth fell open. "That's just a truth dressed up like a dare."

I glared at him. "If you think it's a dare, say aye."

And the ayes had it, no matter how loudly Fabio said nay.

At the end of the trip, we had a good list lined up, including every crazy thing from *do the worm during a slow dance* to *steal the prom queen's crown*. But the dare I was most worried about?

The stupid one I'd thought of earlier. *Tell someone how you really feel about them*.

Whether I was afraid because I didn't want to tell Emerick or because of what he might say to me if I did, I didn't know.

The limo pulled in front of the school, and in a few seconds, we'd have to get out and start the night.

Emerick kept the list since he would be sitting down. We all went into prom, and Emerick and I sat along the edges of the dancefloor, reading over the items.

He took the end of the pen between his lips, and I couldn't help but think of the dare.

Kiss someone.

That would be so easy. And terrifying.

He looked at me, his eyes sliding up from my mouth to meet my gaze. "What about *drink a cup of punch*? That's an easy one."

I nodded, trying to clear my head. "I'll get it." On my way over to the punch table, I tried to decipher what his gaze meant. Had he been looking at my lips, thinking of kissing me too? By the time I brought a cup of the slushy drink back, I still hadn't decided.

He took a drink and smiled. "That was a good one."

I rubbed my fingers together, evaporating the condensation from his cup. "Definitely." I scanned the dares. "Slow dance with someone?"

Emerick pointed at his cast. "Mind swaying along with a cripple?"

I did have a better idea. I bit my lip. "Mind if I try something?"

His eyes widened, and a strobe light caught his nearly black irises. Just slightly, he nodded.

With my heart racing, I settled onto his lap and linked my arms around his shoulders. "This counts, right?"

His chest lifted, and he blew out a breath. "I

think so." It was barely a whisper, but I caught every syllable, the nervous tone behind his words.

The song playing faded to nothing as the thoughts in my head drowned out the lyrics. Me. Emerick. Prom. How had this ever happened?

"You ever think you'd be here with me?" Emerick asked, reading my mind.

I shook my head. "No, but life has a way of surprising me with really good things."

His Adam's apple bobbed. "Yeah?"

"Yeah."

He traced a slow circle on my back with his hand, leaving a trail of warmth behind his fingers. It felt like bathing in fire. Refreshing and terrifying. Cleansing and ruining. If I kept going, I wouldn't be able to turn around to the world of Polo-shirted guys wielding daddy's money like a weapon. This—Emerick—it was so much more real.

Final chords played through a speaker, and even though Emerick and I hadn't gone anywhere, I felt like we were in a totally different place. At least, I was.

He cleared his throat and reached for the paper again. My back felt cool at the absence of his touch.

"What about number thirteen?" he asked.

"Is that the bathroom one?"

He chuckled. "No. Stick an ice cube down some-one's back."

We both turned our eyes to Fabio, where he danced the sprinkler...then acted like he was screwing in a lightbulb with swaying hips...then made a pizza over his shoulders. Grace shuffled back and forth across from him in some weird version of hammer time.

Emerick groaned. "This is just painful."

I smiled at the pair. "They're having fun."

He grinned, a mischievous glint in his eyes. "For now."

Taking care not to hurt Emerick's injured leg, I got up from the chair and walked back over to the punch table, where melting glasses of ice waited by the water pitcher. I took two and walked back to Emerick. By the time I got there, Grace, Fabio, and London were already around him, glancing at the list.

This was my chance.

I snuck closer to Fabio. Closer. Just as Grace noticed me and yelled, I dump a handful of melty ice down Fabio's back. I might have been student body president with straight As, but the way Emerick grinned and high-fived me made me feel more accom-plished than ever.

Fabio glared at me evilly. "Payback's a witch."

Emerick snorted. That probably wasn't the version he usually heard.

I stared right back at Fabio. "Bring it on, lover boy."

He tossed his head, pretending to flip back long, golden hair. "My grandma didn't name me Fabio for nothin'."

A new song played, and Fabio's gaze jerked in Grace's direction. "Are you thinking what I'm thinking?"

She grinned back at him. "Say it on three."

"One two...Cupid Shuffle!"

She shuffled to him in her Converse, and they went to the dancefloor.

London looked at us. "What are you doing waiting here? Find somewhere else to be before Fabio tries to get you back!"

Emerick huffed. "The revenge of Fabio."

But he didn't have time to think about it, because I was already wheeling him toward the hallway. Fabio pulled the worst pranks.

We ran into a chaperone at the door, and I made up a quick excuse about forgetting Emerick's medicine in his locker. We were home free.

It was totally dark in the locker hallways and eerily quiet compared to the pounding music in the gym. But if Emerick kept looking at me like he had earlier, my heart would probably give those speakers a run for their money.

I tried the handle to one of the classrooms, and fortunately, it gave. We slipped into the dark English room, illuminated only by streetlights pouring in through the windows.

I went and sat at a desk, and Emerick wheeled next to me. My breathing was so loud in this room. I tried to still it, but the way Emerick's eyes bored into me, like he was examining me, taking me in...it was hard to keep my body from going haywire.

To break the silence, I said, "Anything on the list I can do in here?"

But then I regretted it for three very big reasons.

Kiss somebody.

Tell someone how you feel.

Hold hands.

Sure, Emerick and I had held hands for like half a second earlier, and it was wonderful, but now, in an empty classroom with no one around, there was no telling where handholding would lead. Not sexually, but emotionally.

Emerick's eyes lifted from the list and met mine. "You want to pick?"

And this was my chance to decide what kind of person I wanted to be—what kind of person I would be with Emerick.

TWENTY-THREE

EMERICK

NORA'S pretty blue eyes looked almost washed out in that dark classroom, but nothing dulled the vulnerability in her gaze. The nervous way she bit her full bottom lip.

Part of me wished she'd just say it. *Kiss me.* But the other half of me, my alter ego, Adam, begged for the chance to come clean. This was ThePerfectStranger, after all. The girl I'd told about missing my dad. Who'd helped me realize I could want something more for my future than a full-time job at my uncle's shop.

Her voice came out a whisper. "Tell someone how you feel about them." Her hands came together on top of the desk, and she fiddled with a little ring on her right hand. A silver band that said *True love waits*.

A purity ring.

Yet another shining reminder of what different worlds we came from. Could I really tell her who I was?

Could she believe we weren't so different after all?

Could I believe the same thing?

God, this whole thing had me messed up. But here was this beautiful girl, sitting across from me and staring at me like I was the moon. Waiting to see the man inside.

I reached out and covered her hands with mine, hiding the ring, but I could still feel it on my palm. The soft skin on her hands sent flames in my chest like I'd never felt before. How could this perfect girl set me on fire? Would she just leave me to ash?

"Nora," I said, and because I was a chicken shit, I said, "if you want me to come clean, you better buy me dinner first."

Her lips fell for a fraction of a second, and my head went spiraling down, down, kicking myself with my messed-up leg because I never wanted to make her do anything but smile. But her smile came back again, and it was radiant.

"I can't exactly buy you dinner," she said. "But I'll make you some." And, get this, she actually pulled out an invisible mixing bowl and acted like she was cooking me something.

I leaned forward and rested my elbows on the desk. "Watchu makin'?"

She looked at me with the practiced eyes of someone who had little kids bug them with that exact question. "Food."

Even my best efforts couldn't crack a resolve like that. "I'm sure I'll love it."

She reached up and tucked a loose curl behind her ear. I swore she just left it out so she could do that. So she could tease me.

Her hand trailed back over her delicate collarbone to the invisible bowl, and then she used an invisible ladle to pour me some.

Like the hopeless case I was, I took an imaginary spoon, lifted a "bite" to my mouth, and went on and on about how good it was. Man, I had it bad.

"Okay," she said. "Tell me about yourself. Something no one else knows."

This would be the perfect chance. But I couldn't. "I got my leather jacket from my grandpa's house after he died. It was his."

Her eyes softened, and she put a hand on my wrist. "Were you close?"

"He was like my dad. I mean, my dad was around, but Grandpa did all the dad stuff Dad didn't do...if that makes sense."

Nora nodded. "My grandma was like that." She

pulled out her clutch and zipped it open, retrieving this little golden pin. "She actually gave this to me before she died." Her fingers wrapped around the pin, and she held it to her chest for a moment before putting it away.

Maybe we were more alike than we thought.

My lips smiled on their own. "What about you? What's your secret?"

This cute, flirty smirk lit up her features. "I guess, now that we've had dinner, I can tell you." She looked down, pausing for so long, I wondered if she would talk again. "All of my secrets aren't really mine anymore."

And I felt like crap, because she was right. My secrets were out there, too, but no one knew they were mine.

She sighed. "I mean, it's still a little embarrassing, but it's nice to have it out there, you know? Like, the pressure is off. Finally. I just..." Her expression turned nervous.

"What?" I asked.

Nora shook her head. "It's just... My privacy wasn't the only thing I lost. I lost one of my best friends."

Just tell her. Tell her she never lost her friend, that Adam had been there for her all along.

But I couldn't. I just gripped her hand, the difference in our coloring so much more apparent in the darkness.

She tried to smile at me, tried on that brave face she had worn a million times before. But now I recognized it for what it was. A cover. Her smile cracked just as quickly as it had come. "I think we should get back down there."

The moment was gone. I nodded.

And just when I least expected it, she leaned over the desk and put her lips to mine. Just for a second. But that was all I needed to know I was completely, irreversibly, hopelessly hooked on Nora Wilson.

Her eyes cut through me, and the smile on her lips cauterized the wound, marking me hers and hers alone. "I had to cross something else off the list."

My gut sank. As I followed her into the hallway, one fear ran through my mind. Was that all it was to her? Something to check off list?

We made it back to the dance and found the other three almost immediately. London was dancing with people from the cheer squad. Grace and Fabio had started a weird dance crew filled with friends doing the sprinkler, not ironically.

After the song, London walked up to us. "You missed it. The kid who won prom king actually gave a speech. And it included a song. And then he kissed on Missy Hamden during the dance."

I scrunched my eyebrows. "Was he drunk?"

"Oh yeah," London said.

Nora snorted. "Good thing Trey couldn't win. Might have missed out on the entertainment."

"Yeah," London said. "You'll have to check Facebook or YouTube tomorrow. I bet someone posted it."

I nodded and pulled my phone out of my pocket to check the time. There was only half an hour left of the dance.

"You should go dance," I told Nora. "Grace and Fabio are showing us up."

Her teeth caught her bottom lip. "Are you sure?"

I smiled. "Go ahead. Come on, it's senior prom. You have to."

She and London jumped into the fray, showing their crew how the starting-the-lawnmower move was done. And because it was dark enough, and I was there as Nora's date, I could watch them without looking like a total creep, even though I kind of was.

God, how had I never noticed Nora or the gentle way she treated all of her friends? The way she tilted her head back when she laughed?

"You with Nora?"

I jerked my head to the side. Trey stood beside me, using every inch of his six-foot-plus-some frame to tower over me in my chair. You know, like a real asshole.

"What's it to you?" I asked.

He scowled in Nora's direction and knelt beside me. "Let me give you a little advice. Friend to friend." He gripped my chair. "Just because you can rent a tux and wash your hair doesn't mean you'll ever be good enough for that girl over there. Even if she'd deluded herself into thinking you're worth more than the shit they use to fertilize her family's yard, she has other people around who know better. You think her dad'll be thrilled about his first-born dating the son of a convict?" He paused, eyeing me, but I didn't speak.

Honestly, I was so pissed, if I spoke I'd yell, and if I yelled, I'd punch him in the toilet bowl he called a mouth.

Trey laughed under his breath. "Yeah, I thought so. Didn't want you forgetting where you came from."

He sauntered off, went and grabbed some girl's ass, but I was already getting my phone out, reading an email Nora had sent me all those weeks ago. I'd saved it because the words had cut me deep.

You are not your parents or your past or what other people think of you. You are who you choose to be when no one's watching.

Well, who I was now was someone in hiding, and I needed to stop. I needed to be honest with the girl who'd been nothing but honest with me from the very start.

Before I could lose my nerve, I made a promise to myself. I was telling Nora tonight. Right after prom. Right after her friends got out of the limo.

Tonight.

The last song of the night was a slow song, and Nora came back to me. Without asking, she settled onto my lap, and it felt good to have her that close. I savored every second of the dance, knowing it could very well be my last with her. Yeah, she missed Adam, but it was Emerick who had kept the secret from her.

Nora lowered her head until her forehead rested against mine, and I closed my eyes, breathing in this moment that smelled like raspberries and mint and perfection like I never had.

"This night's been perfect," she breathed.

I smiled. "Yeah, it has been."

"Thanks for asking me."

"Thanks for saying yes."

A quiet laugh escaped her lips. "You're welcome."

She moved to rest her head on my shoulder, and we just sat like that until the song ended and her friends found us. Then we had to go back out to the limo, even though I could have sat in that gym forever.

After the limo dropped us off, this could all be

over. I would have surgery. Nora would have to go back to all of her responsibilities. We would graduate. God, living in the moment was hard when you knew it could all be ripped away in a second.

We all piled into the limo, and this time, Nora sat right by me, leaned her head on my shoulder.

Grace and London didn't come because they were staying for an after-prom party with the cheerleaders, but Fabio slid in across from us and slouched down in the seat.

"Who won?" he asked.

I pulled the sheet out of my pocket and looked at all the chicken scratch markings. I laughed at the list. "Did you really drop a quarter down someone's underwear."

Fabio laughed tiredly and hung his head. "It wasn't my proudest moment."

I snorted. "Well, it put you over the top. You won by a point. Nora came in second."

Fabio lifted his eyebrows, looking impressed. "Nice job, Nora. Who'd've thunk it."

She rolled her eyes. "I might surprise you."

I pulled Nora in closer under my arm. "Always. In a good way."

She smiled up at me, and Fabio made a gagging sound, but we ignored him, too busy doing lame couple shit like looking into each other's eyes. But it didn't feel lame. It felt amazing to have those baby blues turned on me.

The limo driver came to a stop.

"This is me," Fabio said.

I broke eye contact with Nora long enough to give him a two-finger wave. He was actually pretty cool. He and Wolf might get along, now that Wolf was clean.

But the limo driver shut the door behind him, and this was the time.

"Nora," I said, before I could lose my nerve and back out, "I have to tell you something."

Her eyes were wide, worried.

It hit me that she might not believe me if I just came out and said it, so I reached into my pocket, took out my phone, and replied to her email.

To: Nora Wilson
From: ADAM
Dear Nora,

Thank you for being one of the best friends a guy could have. I hope you'll still be my friend after this.

Signed,
Emerick

TWENTY-FOUR

NORA

ADAM'S RINGTONE sounded from my clutch, and I reached for it. But my fingers never made it to the zipper, because my mind finally caught up.

Emerick's phone.

Adam's ringtone.

Emerick needing to tell me something.

Adam's ringtone.

I stared at the guy sitting beside me, his phone lowered with his thumbs still on the scratched screen. How many messages had those thumbs sent me?

He gazed back at me, a wounded intensity in his eyes like I'd never seen before. Emerick was Adam. Adam was Emerick.

My mouth opened and closed, but no words came out. I'd thought of a million things I wanted to say to Adam if we ever met, but I'd never thought of what

I'd say to him if he was my prom date, my class partner...someone I'd never imagined could write all the amazing advice Adam had.

Emerick's eyes pleaded with me. "Say something."

My eyes stung, and my throat got tight. "What do you want me to say?"

Here was the guy who I'd shared some of my deepest hopes and dreams with. Who'd helped me get over Trey. Who'd said we could never meet. And I couldn't help the way this confused sensation was ripping through my chest, tearing me apart.

Emerick looked at his hands. "I don't know."

I waited for him to say more, but he didn't, and my confusion turned to anger. "That's it?"

He dropped this bomb on me and all he had to say was *I don't know*? There had to be more. Some explanation of how he could sit next to me every day after those emails went public and not say a single word.

But when he still didn't speak, I said, "Why didn't you tell me?"

He hung his head and finally turned those doleful brown eyes on me. "If I told you, I wouldn't have been able to graduate."

I folded my arms across my chest. "Seriously?" No matter how earnest he looked, the humiliated, rejected, lonely part of me couldn't believe him. "What changed?"

"Mrs. Arthur said you deserved to know."

I snorted derisively. Whoever this person was that had inhabited my body was keeping me sitting up straight, being strong, not the pathetic open wound I felt like on the inside. "Mrs. Arthur was right," I said. "I did deserve to know. You've been lying to me, taking me out, and it wasn't fair because you knew who I was, and I didn't know who you were."

The limo slowed down, and I saw the panic on Emerick's face. He didn't want me to leave, but that just made me want to leave even more.

He put his hand on my arm. "You knew me."

We came to a stop, and I pulled back. "No, I knew Adam."

Before the driver could open the door, before Emerick could look at me like that for a second longer, I got out of the limo and ran down the side-walk toward my house, crying, because my biggest fantasy had turned into my worst nightmare.

"Nora!" Emerick called, but I was already to the door.

I stepped inside and took a deep, calming breath. Thankfully, no one was up in the living room, but I saw the light on in the kitchen. Mom probably waited up for me.

"Nora?" she called.

"I'm home," I said. "I'm going to head upstairs and change."

Without waiting for her, I slipped off my shoes and padded up the stairs as fast as I could. In my room, I flipped on the lights, changed, and hung my dress back on the silky hanger. Things were so different from when I'd slipped it on earlier that evening.

I still couldn't wrap my mind around the news. Emerick was Adam? I mean, Emerick was sweet and kind, even if he was rough around the edges. He didn't talk much, but when he did, it counted.

Wasn't that what I'd liked about Adam?

But that didn't change the fact that Emerick had known and asked me out. Here I thought I was going out with my social studies partner, and he'd known he was dating ThePerfectStranger.

I buried myself under my covers and even put a pillow over my face, trying to drown out all the conflicting thoughts in my mind. I should be thrilled. Part of me was. What was wrong with me?

My phone chimed with Adam's ringtone. Emerick's ringtone.

But I didn't need to be confused right now. No, right now, I needed to fall into darkness, to forget what Emerick's lips felt like on mine.

I turned off the phone and breathed deeply until I fell into a heavy sleep full of alphabet soup dreams, each more confusing than the last.

Dad nudged me awake the next morning. "We've got to get going, Nora Bug. Thirty minutes until we leave."

With my phone still off, I got ready, my thoughts from earlier hitting me stronger than ever before. I walked downstairs, finding everyone in the living room. Amie was already in her ballet company's sweats, and the younger girls looked like they were drowsy enough to fall back asleep the second they got in the car, but they were still dressed.

Dad waved his arms impatiently. "Come on, Nora. We've got to drop Amie off on time."

Amie tapped her foot impatiently.

"Sorry," I mumbled and yawned.

We all got into the van, and I leaned my bucket seat back.

"Stop!" Esther cried.

I looked back at her, her drooping eyes. "I'm not touching you; it's fine."

She kicked the headrest. "Move!"

Edith jerked her little head up, seconds to a meltdown.

Mom glanced back. "Push your chair up."

I glared between the two of them. "She's four, but whatever." I lifted it up and closed my eyes.

What a mess. What a giant, crummy crap hole I'd made for myself. I wished I'd just had some sense and talked to a counselor. Someone who actually couldn't reveal all my secrets. Someone who couldn't break my heart.

Was that what Emerick had done?

He couldn't do that if I didn't care about him.

Mom's words hit me harder than ever. *You'll have to decide what compromises you're willing to make.*

Adam—Emerick had broken my heart, but hadn't he done so much more than that? He'd given up countless evenings talking to a stranger he couldn't ever meet. He'd held my cyber hand through a horrible relationship and breakup. He'd listened and understood and kept my secret about my dad, even when letting it out probably could have earned him a fair amount of money. Which his family probably needed.

Suddenly, our car felt too small to hold these emotions raging in my mind. I had to let them out, to see Emerick face-to-face. After the hurt look he'd had the day before, an email wouldn't be enough.

Dad pulled into the parking lot in front of the building where the charter bus waited for Amie's team, exhaust pouring out behind it.

"Good luck, kiddo," he said to her. "We'll be watching."

She smiled tiredly. "Thanks."

"Knock 'em dead," I whispered.

This time her eyes crinkled. "KO on the dance floor."

Once she was out of the van, I leaned forward. "Mom, Dad, can I stay home? I'm...not feeling well."

Dad looked at me in the rearview. "We told you when you went to prom you'd be coming to this. Wilsons stick to their commitments."

Anger rose up in my chest at him. Wilsons stuck to their commitments. Unless the promise was 'til death do us part. "Do you want me to throw up in the van?" I really could have, from disgust alone.

His eyes set. "I guess that's a risk I'm willing to take."

I wanted to scream, to jump out of the van and run, but what would that accomplish? Plus, I did want to be there for Amie.

But Monday morning, I would be outside the school, waiting for Emerick. I would be there for him like he'd been there for me. I just hoped it wasn't too late.

TWENTY-FIVE
EMERICK

SEVEN HOURS OF SLEEP LATER, and I still felt like my heart had been carved out of my chest with a rusty spoon. Nora's face, full of betrayal, seared itself into my mind. It was all I could see when I closed my eyes.

I'd been through enough, but I'd never imagined how bad it would be to see her running away. Literally running. She couldn't get away from me fast enough.

I brought my fist down on the bed next to me. I should have told her the second I knew it was her. Nora was a good person—she'd never have snitched, especially when she knew the stakes.

Just another way she was too damn good for me.

The garage door opened, and Aunt Linda poked her head in. "I'm taking the boys to a movie, but

Janie doesn't want to go. You'll be around to keep an eye on her?"

I stared at the rafters. "Sure."

"Thanks. She's reading, so she'll be good for hours." She chuckled. "See you soon."

"No problem." I didn't want to leave this bed anyway. Didn't deserve to go anywhere.

My phone chimed, and I dug through the covers, trying to find it.

Why the hell did blankets always become the Bermuda Triangle when you were looking for something?

My hand finally connected with something hard. I pulled the blanket up until my phone fell on the cement floor. Reaching for it, I stared at the cracked screen, wishing more than anything the message was from Nora instead of Wolf.

But there it was.

Wolf: How was prom?

Wolf: Get some action?

Eggplant emoji.

Water emoji.

Peach emoji.

Emerick: STOP

Panty emoji.

Another eggplant.

Emerick: God, I need to find some new friends.

Wolf: rofl

Wolf: ???

Emerick: It was fine until I fkn blew it

Wolf: ;)

Emerick: Don't be gross

Wolf: What happened

Emerick: I don't wanna talk about it

Wolf: ok

Wolf: surgerys tomorrow right

Emerick: don't wanna talk about that either.

Wolf: Meet me outside in 10

Emerick: No. Gotta watch Janie.

Wolf: Bring the kid.

I rolled over on my bed, shoved my face into my pillow, and roared.

What Wolf didn't get was that going out and jumping in a pond wouldn't get me past this. I wasn't trying to get my mind off school or work. This was another person. The woman I... I couldn't say the word. That would make it too real.

Pathetic.

His engine fired in the driveway, and he honked.

The garage door opened, and Janie poked her head in, looking like a little, annoyed version of her mom. "Can you tell your friend to be quiet? I'm trying to read."

I glanced at the book in her hand. "You reading romance?"

She hid it behind her back.

Wolf honked again.

"Tell him to be quiet!" she cried.

I grunted. "Put that book down." I got out of bed, hopped to my dresser, and threw a shirt on. "Come on."

She put some flip flops on and followed me out the garage door, out into Wolf's El Camino, which he was actually keeping clean lately.

Janie got into the middle seat. "We have a doorbell, you know?"

I lifted my eyebrows at Wolf, and he laughed. "I'll keep that in mind, kid."

She scowled at him. Apparently, I wasn't the only one in a shit mood today.

Wolf took off down the road. "So what happened last night?"

I glanced back at Janie, her nose already buried in some book with a shirtless man on the cover. She was only ten. What the hell did she want to do with a book like that?

I made a mental note to tell Aunt Linda to hide her books better and sighed. "I blew things with Nora. She won't talk to me."

Wolf glanced at me. "You gonna piss and moan about it, or you wanna do something?"

I glared at him. "I tried texting her. She won't answer."

"You call her?"

"Straight to voicemail."

He frowned. "What's plan B?"

Janie piped up from behind her book. "Ice cream."

A smirk cracked Wolf's expression.

I shrugged. "You heard the girl."

He drove to a Sonic, and we got out of the car. I hopped to a table with Janie holding onto my arm, making sure I didn't fall over.

We ordered and sat around.

Janie shoved my shoulder. "Why are you moping around?"

Coming from a ten-year-old? Ouch. "What do you mean?"

She gave me a no-nonsense stare. Yeah, she might have been a ten-year-old, but she knew a thing or two. Or three.

I sighed. "Prom didn't end the way I wanted it to."

"What happened?"

Wolf leaned in.

Another sigh. "She figured out who I really was."

And that was all I could say, because even Wolf didn't know about the column. Living with my dad had made keeping secrets so natural, I didn't even know how to be open, and I didn't want to blame my problems on daddy issues, but I didn't want to ignore my problems either.

I looked Wolf right in the eye. "Snitches get stiches."

He just looked confused.

"You can keep a secret?"

He looked at Janie. "If she can, I can."

She nodded.

I looked around the empty outdoor area, the sparse parking stalls, making sure no one would overhear us. "I'm Adam. I'm the one who's been writing the advice column."

Wolf shook his head. "You're shitting me."

I tilted my head toward Janie.

Wolf's lips pulled back. "Sorry...Seriously?"

I nodded. "And you can't tell anyone, or I won't graduate."

An employee wobbled out on skates and set our ice cream down. Thankfully, she was more focused on staying upright than on us.

Wolf covered his mouth with his hand. "That means Nora was..."

I nodded.

"What?" Janie asked.

I shoved my spoon in my sundae, trying to shove down all the feelings Nora had dragged up the night before. "Nora was writing me as the advice columnist, but she didn't know that it was me. And I told her last night."

Janie's eyes widened. "She wasn't happy about it?"

I shoved a spoonful of ice cream in my mouth and shook my head. Could brain freezes freeze thoughts too? I'd like for all these bad feelings to stop.

Wolf patted my back. "She'll come around."

I looked right at him. "You mean that?" I wanted to believe him. More than anything.

He nodded, and Janie took my free hand, saying, "If she doesn't, she doesn't deserve you."

My throat got tight, and I ducked my head down so I could wipe away the proof of how much this hurt.

Janie studied me. "Got something in your eyes?"

Wolf snorted. "Yeah. Some tears."

"Whatever." I shoved him, but I was laughing.

Maybe ice cream couldn't fix everything, but at least I wasn't alone.

Ma, Uncle Ken, and I sat in the orthopedic surgery

lobby. These places were the worst. You didn't know whether you'd get some weird shit from touching the chairs or whether the old people hobbling around in front of you would fall over or not.

And yeah, it didn't help that Ma wouldn't stop wringing her hands and that I'd have to go in for a second surgery on my leg, be put under, and then go through months of rehab just so I could walk with a limp.

My phone went off.

Wolf: Good luck man.

Emerick: Thanks

I looked at the time. In three minutes, the first bell would ring. Nora would sit down in homeroom with the rest of our classmates. She'd start her day at Warr Acres High School, knowing her future was set. Whether she forgave me or not, she'd have her perfect friends, her family.

And what did I have? A list of rejection emails in my inbox longer than my right arm.

I went to my inbox again, wishing there would be a message from Nora. Something to say she'd changed her mind this weekend. But nothing.

"Emerick Turner?" The little Mexican nurse said it like E-mare-ick, but I still stood up.

My phone went off again, probably something from Wolf, but I left it in my pocket. It was time.

TWENTY-SIX
NORA

I STOOD by the school entrance, watching everyone race past me to make it to class before the tardy bell rang. Wolf had walked in without Emerick earlier, and I wished I'd been smart enough to ask why he hadn't given Emerick a ride.

Emerick had texted me after prom. Apologies, asking me to talk. And now that I wanted to, he was nowhere to be found. Where was he, and why wasn't he replying to my message?

Then it dawned on me. He was having surgery.

The tardy bell rang, and I did something I had never done before. I walked back out to my car and skipped school.

He'd been at St. Anthony's before, so I crossed my fingers and drove across town to the hospital. At the front desk, I asked if he was there.

Yes, he was.

No, I couldn't see him. He was in surgery.

No, they couldn't tell me how it was going.

Yes, I could wait in the waiting room.

I readjusted my purse over my shoulder and went to the elevator, wondering how I had been so stupid. Emerick was in surgery right now, had been anesthetized without knowing where we stood. Who knew how long it would take for him to wake up. Or if he would.

As I got on the elevator and pushed the button, I tried to remind myself of my faith in the medical system. In God. But that all went away when I reached the orthopedic surgery waiting room.

There were several people there, and none looked as nervous as the two back in the corner. They were the only black people there. The woman had her arms wrapped around her middle, bent forward like she was holding herself together. The man next to her had his hand on her back and his eyes closed, his lips moving.

Even though we were in a public space, I felt like I was intruding on them, walking in on something intimate and private.

I didn't know whether to leave or introduce myself, but sitting down in one of the empty chairs seemed wrong.

The woman looked up and met my stare. She had Emerick's eyes—dark, round orbs that could cut through you and comfort you without warning.

"Hi," I said, stepping closer.

The guy looked me up and down curiously, but it was Emerick's mom who spoke. "Do you know Rick?"

Feeling more nervous than ever, I nodded. "We went to prom together."

I watched her expression to see if he'd told her anything, but she just smiled for a fraction of a second and nodded. "You can sit with us, baby."

Despite myself, I smiled. "Thank you." I didn't deserve it, but I could already see Emerick in her. I hoped he would be just as forgiving.

She caught me up on the situation. Right now, they were taking off the external fixator—removing screws they'd used to stabilize his leg. And then he'd move on to a regular cast. She said he would be done in about an hour, if all worked as planned.

A doctor walked out and called, "Turner."

We all stood up, and he came over. He looked young for a surgeon, but I didn't mind the thought of Emerick being worked on by some kind of prodigy.

He grinned at us. "Everything went well."

My phone went off, and my cheeks heated. "I'm so sorry." I reached into my purse and pushed the button to silence it without looking at the screen. It was probably my mom, calling because she found out I hadn't shown up to class.

The doctor nodded and continued. "The bones are healing nicely, and we have a new cast on." He chuckled. "Actually, after the nurse got his things for him, he was shooing us out of the room so he could make a call."

My eyes widened, and I dug back into my purse. One missed call from Emerick.

The three adults watched me, smiling.

The doctor looked between the three of us. "You're welcome to go back and see him."

I started back, but suddenly realized I didn't know his room number. And it was probably weird for his not-even girlfriend to see him first.

"Sorry," I said. "I'll wait here while you all visit."

His mom smiled, relieved, happy. "That's alright, baby girl. We'll talk to the doc while you go back."

"Room 205," the doctor said.

"Right."

But now, on my way back to the room, my heart beat faster than ever before. Emerick had called me. He'd wanted to talk again. I might have been upset at first, but now I had to reckon for my actions.

The sign beside me read 204. Only a few more

steps before I'd come face-to-face with Emerick, the guy who'd had my heart before I'd even seen his face.

Outside the door, I heard him talking. "I want to talk to you about all of this. I want to make it right. Just call me. Please."

Before I lost my nerve, I stepped into the room. "Emerick?"

He jerked his head up, and those eyes landed on me. Those eyes that saw right through me. He lowered the phone to his lap, hit the end button. "You came here?"

I nodded. "I needed to tell you what I should have Saturday."

Emerick stared at me, his eyes wide open and totally vulnerable for the first time. "No, I owe you an—"

I held up my hand. "Can I go first?"

His full lips came together, and he nodded.

Taking in a deep breath, I stepped closer to the bed, stared at his hands in his lap. I took one in mine, watching our fingers come together, the contrast in our skin tones, the roughness of his palm that still hung on from how hard he'd worked.

I held our intertwined hands to my chest and rested my chin on our laced fingers. "Emerick. Adam."

He smiled slightly, but his eyes lit up.

"I know you," I said. "I know you're rough around the edges and cuss and that your dad's in jail."

His chin tipped down, but I lifted his head with my free hand, so he had to turn those eyes on me.

"I didn't finish," I said, and he just waited, looking so conflicted my heart hurt for him. I held his hand even tighter. "I know you're kind. And you listen. And you have a heart for helping other people. And that you're the most amazing prom date I've ever had. The thought of not emailing you anymore, not talking to you anymore...I can't fathom that. Because I need you. As my friend. As more. If you'll have me."

His lips trembled before he pressed them together, and he looked over his shoulder, pressing his cheek into my hand. And then he didn't say anything, just pulled me into his chest, breathing heavy.

I stayed there, feeling my heart slow. This was how things should be between us, where I needed to be.

He took a deep breath. "I'm so sorry I couldn't tell you."

I shook my head against the rough fabric of his hospital gown. "I understand."

Tears leaked out my eyes, and I squeezed them shut. I'd been a mess when I'd first emailed him, and I was a mess now, for completely different reasons.

We all had our flaws, and I'd just been lucky enough to share mine with him.

When I pulled back, he took my face in both of his hands, studying me like I was the most beautiful thing he'd ever seen.

I took him in, really, for the first time. The scar over his eyebrow, the way his lashes curled up. The full curve of his lips and how they turned from deep brown to pink where they came together.

Slowly, he brought my face closer and pressed those lips to mine, sweeping me into this new world where the guy in the leather jacket and the student body president could be so much more than strangers passing the hallway.

That was the thing I was starting to learn. Some of the people I'd idolized—my dad and Trey—they were nothing but a pretty picture covered in flaws. And some people you thought you'd never connect with might just be exactly what you needed.

EPILOGUE

EMERICK

I WALKED into Mrs. Arthur's office for the last time, maybe ever. All the bobbleheads were still there—still annoying as hell—but the space felt different now.

She looked up from her computer screen and smiled. "Emerick. I'm just finishing up some paperwork." She clacked a few more keys on the keyboard. "Congratulations, by the way."

I grinned back at her and shifted the plastic bag holding my graduation cap and gown to my other hand so I could slide the laptop bag off my shoulder and give it to her. "I brought this back."

"Thank you." She nodded toward the chair. "You can set it there."

I put it down, and this awkward feeling hung in

the air. How did you thank a guidance counselor who gave you the worst and ultimately best assignment of your life? "I—um. Thanks. For everything."

She seemed to get it. "Is Nora waiting for you?"

I shook my head. "I'm heading to her place after this."

"Ah." Mrs. Arthur nodded just like her bobble-heads and reached behind her desk, pulling out two wrapped gifts. "I got these for you." She handed me the smaller one. "Open this first."

My ears felt warm. Teachers never gave me presents. Still, I took it and peeled back the paper, then opened the brown cardboard box. Inside was the broken Bob Stoops, the one Nora had ripped in half.

I chuckled and grinned at her.

"I thought you'd like that." She smiled and handed me the other gift. "Now this one."

I ripped the paper and flipped open the leather scrapbook. The pages held every article I'd written over the semester, pages and pages of lost students and my words helping them through. My throat got tight thinking of all the pain this scrapbook held.

"Go to the last page," she said.

I did, and my eyes fell upon the last column I'd written for the paper, a note to the student body.

"I think you should read it again," she said.
And I did.

Dear WAHS,

Adam here. You might be surprised by this, but when I started the column, I wasn't exactly ready to give advice. Honestly, I thought the whole thing was kind of dumb. I had this chip on my shoulder thinking everything I was going through had to be worse than you guys. That your problems weren't real. But then I started hearing from you, reading your emails. I started learning what other people have to deal with every day.

None of us get out of high school without scars, whether you're the student body president or a fly-under-the-radar guy like me. I think the thing that matters is what you do with those scars. You could try and pass your pain onto other people, or you could be honest—with yourself and others— and reach out. And then use what you've learned to help someone else.

I know this column was meant to help all of you, but you helped me. You showed me what it meant to be vulnerable and open. You taught me how to heal. You taught me how to thank the people who helped you up when you thought you'd be on the ground forever.

So thank you. I'll never be able to say thank you enough. If you want to keep hearing from me, you should check out the Norman Transcript. *That's where I'll be writing next. This might be my last column here, but I hope to hear from you again soon, not as a columnist, but as a friend.*

Signed,
Adam.

When I blinked away the mist in my eyes and looked up, Mrs. Arthur was holding up a certificate.

The National High School Newspaper Association awards "Best Advice Column" to the WAHS Ledger.

I stared at her. "I don't know what to say."

"You don't have to say anything," she said. "You earned it." She wrapped me in a hug. "Stay in touch."

I promised her I would.

As I walked out of her office, holding the best gifts I'd ever gotten, I couldn't stop thinking about the Bob Stoops bobblehead and how much I was like him.

The advice column—Nora—had ripped me in half

and made me into something even better than I ever could have imagined.

***

To read more quirky romance for the young at heart, download Fabio vs. the Friend Zone by Kelsie Stelting.

THE END

Thank you for reading *Dear Adam*!
Continue reading in The Pen Pal Romance Series by
grabbing a copy of Fabio vs. the Friend Zone.
To be alerted about new releases, visit
www.kelsiestelting.com and sign up for the email
newsletter.

ALSO BY KELSIE STELTING

The Pen Pal Romance Series

Dear Adam

Coming soon

Fabio vs. the Friend Zone

Sincerely Cinderella

The Texas Star Series

Lonesome Skye: Book One

Becoming Skye: Book Two

Loving Skye: Book Three

Always Anika

Abi and the Boy Next Door

YA Contemporary Romance Anthology

The Art of Taking Chances

The Texas Sun Series

All the Things He Left Behind

Unfair Catch: Savannah's Story 1

Anything But Yes: Savannah's Story 2

Nonfiction

Raising the West

ACKNOWLEDGMENTS

I probably don't say thank you enough, so I'm glad every book has a section where I can spell out the names of everyone who's helped me along the way. *Dear Adam* couldn't have made it into the world without help from the family, friends, and professionals who have supported me either in my career as a writer or on this project specifically.

I'm thankful to God for giving me the talent, the skills, the need to put words on paper.

My husband, for being a constant source of support, laughter, and unexpected/unconventional romance.

My parents, for telling me I could be anything I dreamed.

My siblings, for being my best friends and advocates.

The YA chicks, for their expert advice and friendship.

My editor, Tricia Harden, for taking such care with my stories and making the effort to truly know my characters.

Jenny with Seedlings for her expert, beautiful cover design.

Everyone I encountered at the Oklahoma Capitol, for their kind stewardship and willingness to answer my questions, no matter how strange.

Each of my advanced readers, for their love of literature and taking the time to support my work.

The members of my Readers Club for their friendship. Interacting with them day to day is a joy.

Finally, I'm thankful for you, the reader. Thank you for taking the time to share my world. I promise I worked to make it as wonderful as possible. You deserve only the very best.

AUTHOR'S NOTE

Almost two years ago now, I was sitting on the couch in my living room, crying, talking on the phone with my husband, and telling him that I needed to stop writing and go to nursing school. I remember saying, "There's such a need in mental health nursing, and me struggling as a writer isn't helping anyone."

Being the wonderful man that he is, he offered me his full support with whatever I decided to choose. Because ultimately, it was my choice.

After we hung up, I set my phone down beside me, pulled out my computer, and tried to get lost in my Facebook newsfeed. Almost immediately, I got a message from someone I hadn't heard from in eight years. She told me that she loved my writing and that it reminded her of John Green's style. At the very end, she said, keep writing.

I read the message again and began crying. What she didn't know was that in the cubicle at my job in data entry, I had a sticky note that said, "John Green used to work as a typist."

I don't know how, but that message reached me right at one of the biggest crossroads in my life. I'm so thankful to that friend, and to God, who I believe gave her that push to message me, right when I needed it.

I knew all of the shoulds in my life. I graduated summa cum laude with an honors degree. I had a heart for people and knew I could do well in school. There were people out there who could use me as a nurse. That was my should.

But my calling?

That was telling stories.

What I hadn't realized was that I could help people just as much through my writing, as well as myself. I needed storytelling to get me through times harder than I ever could have imagined, and it's helped readers do the same. Writing has brought me so many friends and opportunities I never would have otherwise known.

I think Emerick and I struggled with the same thing. Duty to others vs. the frivolous natures of our dreams. What we both forgot is that sometimes, the person we need to help is ourselves. Serving others does nothing if we do it without joy and passion—if we do it from a place of "should" rather than "must."

The only problem? Sometimes choosing must is scary. It might look crazy to those around you. And sometimes it's reckless, because it requires a leap of faith. With writing, I had to jump and trust that I would find my readers, my place in the writing community.

Must doesn't mean you lose all practicality and concern for others. It means you become the best, most fulfilled version of yourself, so you have more to give.

You might be choosing between should and must yourself. If you are, I hope you'll have the courage to face whatever lies ahead and give the best of yourself to others. You deserve it.

ABOUT THE AUTHOR

Kelsie Stelting grew up in the middle of nowhere (also known as western Kansas). Her rural upbringing taught her how to get her hands dirty and work hard for what she believes in. Plus, not having neighbors in a 10-mile radius as a child and traveling the world as an adult made her develop a pretty active imagination. Kelsie loves writing honest fiction that readers can vacation in, as well as traveling, volunteering, ice cream, loving on her family, and soaking up just a little too much sun wherever she can find it.

To connect with Kelsie, email her at kelsie@kelsiestelting.com or visit her on social media. She loves hearing from readers!

facebook.com/kelsiesteltingcreative

twitter.com/kelsiestelting

instagram.com/kelsiestelting